ICE AND FIRE

By the same author

Nonfiction

Woman Hating
Our Blood: Prophecies and Discourses on Sexual Politics
Pornography: Men Possessing Women
Right-wing Women:
    The Politics of Domesticated Females

Fiction

the new womans broken heart: short stories

ICE AND FIRE

A Novel
by
Andrea Dworkin

First published in 1986 by
Stoddart Publishing Co. Limited
34 Lesmill Road
Toronto, Canada
M3B 2T6

Published in England by
Martin Secker & Warburg Limited
54 Poland Street
London W1V 3DF

Canadian Cataloguing in Publication

Dworkin, Andrea
   Ice and fire
   I. Title.
   PS3554.W85I24 1986   813'.54   C86–093108–0
   ISBN 0–7737–2084–7

Printed and bound in Great Britain
by Billings & Son Ltd,
Hylton Road, Worcester

For Elaine Markson

Neither weep nor laugh but understand.

Spinoza

*

I have two first memories.

The sofa is green with huge flowers imprinted on it, pink and beige and streaks of yellow or brown, like they were painted with a wide brush to highlight the edges and borders of the flowers. The sofa is deep and not too long, three cushions, the same green. The sofa is against a wall in the living room. It is our living room. Nothing in it is very big but we are small and so the ceilings are high and the walls tower, unscalable, and the sofa is immense, enough width and depth to burrow in, to get lost in. My brother is maybe two. I am two years older. He is golden, a white boy with yellow hair and blue eyes: and happy. He has a smile that lights up the night. He is beautiful and delicate and divine. Nothing has set in his face yet, not fear, not malice, not anger, not sorrow: he knows no loss or pain: he is delicate and happy and intensely beautiful, radiance and delight. We each get a corner of the sofa. We crouch there until the referee, father always, counts to three: then we meet in the middle and tickle and tickle until one gives up or the referee says to go back to our corners because a round is over. Sometimes we are on the floor, all three of us, tickling and wrestling, and laughing past when I hurt until dad says stop. I remember the great print flowers, I remember crouching and waiting to hear three, I remember the great golden smile of the little boy, his yellow curls cascading as we roll and roll.

The hospital is all light brown outside, stone, lit up by electric lights, it is already dark out, and my grandfather and I are outside, waiting for my dad. He comes running. Inside I am put in a small room. A cot is set up for him. My tonsils will come out. Somewhere in the hospital is my mother. I think all night long that she must be in the next room. I tap on the wall, sending secret signals. She has been away from home for a long time. The whole family is in the hospital now, my father with me: I don't know where my brother is—is he born yet?

7

He is somewhere for sure, and my mother is somewhere, probably in the next room. I remember flowered wallpaper. I haven't seen my mother for a very long time and now I am coming to where she is, I expect to see her, I am close to her now, here, in the same hospital, she is near, somewhere, here. I never see her but I am sure she is lying in bed happy to be near me on the other side of the wall in the very next room. She must be happy to know I am here. Her hair was long then, black, and she was young. My father sleeps in the hospital room, in the bed next to mine.

*

The street was home, but, oh, these were kind streets, the streets of children, real children. The houses were brick row houses, all the same, two cement flights of stairs outside, the outside steps, from the sidewalk. The lawns were hills sloping down the height of one flight of steps, the lower one, to the sidewalk. There was a landing between flights. Some of us had patios: the big cement truck came, the huge tumbler turning round and round, and the cement was poured out and flattened down, and sticks marked the edges until it dried. Others had some flowers: next door there were shabby roses, thorns. Each house was the same, two floors, on the first floor a living room, dining room, and tiny kitchen; up a tall flight of stairs three bedrooms, two big, one tiny, a bathroom, a closet. The stairs were the main thing: up and down on endless piggyback rides on daddy's back: up to bed with a piggyback ride, up and down one more time, the greatest ride had a story to go with it about riding horses or piggies going to market; up the stairs on daddy's back and then into bed for the rest of the fabulous story; and I would try to get him to do it again and again, up and down those stairs, and a story. Each house had one family, all the houses were in a row, but two doors were right next to each other above the cement steps so those were the closest neighbors. The adults, mostly the women, would sit on chairs up by their doors, or sit on the steps up by the doors talking and visiting and watching the children, and the children of all the houses would converge in the street to play. If you looked at it you would see dismal brick row houses all the same at the top of two flights of cement steps out in the wea-

8

ther. But if you were a child, you would see that the adults were far away, and that the street stretched into a million secret hidden places. There were parked cars to hide behind and under and telephone poles, the occasional tree, secret valleys at the bottoms of lawns, and the mysterious interiors of other people's houses across the way. And then the backs of the houses made the world bigger, more incredible yet. There were garages back there, a black asphalt back alley and back doors and places to hang clothes on a line and a million places to hide, garbage cans, garages half open, telephone poles, strange dark dirty places, basements. Two blocks behind us in the back there was a convent, a huge walled-in place all verdant with great trees that hid everything: and so our neighborhood turned gothic and spooky and we talked of children captured and hidden inside: and witches. Outside there were maybe twenty of us, all different ages but all children, boys and girls, and we played day after day and night after night, well past dark: hide-and-seek, Red Rover Red Rover, statue, jump rope, hopscotch, giant steps, witch. One summer we took turns holding our breath to thirty and then someone squeezed in our stomachs and we passed out or got real dizzy. This was the thing to do and we did it a million times. There were alleys near one or two of the houses suddenly breaking into the brick row and linking the back ways with the front street and we ran through them: we ran all over, hiding, seeking, making up new games. We divided into teams. We played giant steps. We played Simon Says. Then the boys would play sports without us, and everything would change. We would taunt them into playing with us again, going back to the idyllic, all together, running, screaming, laughing. The girls had dolls for when the boys wouldn't let us play and we washed their hair and set it outside together on the steps. We played poker and canasta and fish and old maid and gin rummy and strip poker. When babies, we played in a sandbox, until it got too small and we got too big. When bigger, we roller-skated. One girl got so big she went out on a date: and we all sat on the steps across the street and watched her come out in a funny white dress with a red flower pinned on it and a funny-looking boy was with her. We were listless that night, not knowing whether to play hide-and-seek or statue. We told nasty stories about the girl in the white dress with the date and wouldn't play with her sister who was like us, not a teenager. Something was wrong. Statue wasn't fun and hide-and-seek got boring too. I watched my house right across the street while the others watched the girl on the date. Intermittently we played statue, bored. Someone had to swing someone else around and then suddenly let them go and however they landed was how they had to stay, like a statue, and everyone had to guess what they were—like a ballet dancer or the Statue of Liberty. Whoever guessed what the statue was got to be turned around and be the new statue. Sometimes just two people played and everybody else would sit around and watch for any little movement and heckle and guess what the person was being a statue of. We were mostly girls by now, playing statue late at night. I watched my house across the street because the doctor had come, the man in the dark suit with the black bag and the dour expression and the unpleasant voice who never spoke except to say something bad and I had been sent outside, I had not wanted to leave the house, I had been ordered to, all the lights were out in the house, it was so dark, and it was late for them to let me out but they had ordered me to go out and play, and have a good time they said, and my mother was in the bedroom with the door closed, and lying down I was sure, not able to move, something called heart failure, something like not being able to breathe, something that bordered on death, it had happened before, I was a veteran, I sat on the steps watching the house while the girl in the white dress stood being laughed at with her date and I had thoughts about death that I already knew I would remember all my life and someday write down: death is someone I know, someone who is dressed exactly like the doctor and carries the same black bag and comes at night and is coming tonight to get mother, and then I saw him come, pretending to be the doctor, and I thought well this is it she will die tonight I know but the others don't because they go on dates or play statue and I'm more mature and so they don't know these things that I know because I live in a house where death comes all the time, suddenly in the night, suddenly in the day, suddenly in the middle of sleeping, suddenly in the middle of a meal, there is death: mother is sick, we've called the doctor, I know death is on the way.

The streetlights lit up the street. The brick was red, even at night. The girl on the date had a white dress with a red corsage. We sat across the street, near our favorite telephone pole for hide-and-seek, and played statue on and off. I always had a home out there, on the steps, behind the cars, near the telephone pole.

*

Inside the woman was dying. Outside we played witch.

The boys chased the girls over the whole block from front to back. They tried to catch a girl. When they caught her they put her in a wooden cage they had built or found and they raised the cage up high on a telephone pole, miles and miles above the ground, with rope, and they left her hanging there. She was the witch. Then they let her down when they wanted to. After she begged and screamed enough and they wanted to play again or do something else.

You were supposed to want them to want to catch you. They would all run after one girl and catch her and put her in the cage and raise it up with the rope high, high on the telephone pole out in the back where the adults didn't see. Then they would hold the cage in place, the girl inside it screaming, four or five of them holding her weight up there in the wooden cage, or they would tie the rope to something and stand and watch.

When they picked you it meant you were popular and fast and hard to catch.

*

When we played witch all the girls screamed and ran as fast as they could. They ran from all the boys and ran so fast and so far that eventually you would run into some boy somewhere but all the boys had decided who they were going to catch so the boy you would run into accidentally would just pass you by and not try to catch you and capture you and put you in the cage.

*

Everyone wanted to be caught and was terrified to be caught. The cage was wooden and had pieces missing and broken. The rope was just a piece of heavy rope one of the boys found somewhere or sometimes even just a piece of clothesline stolen from a backyard. You could hang there for as long as an hour and the boys would threaten to leave you there and all the girls would come and watch. And you would feel ashamed. To be caught or not to be caught.

*

When we played witch it was always the boys against the girls and the boys always chased the girls and it was a hard chase and we ran places we had never seen before and hid in places we were afraid of. There was the street with the row houses facing into it and then there were the back ways behind the houses, and the distance between the back ways and the front street connected by an occasional alley between the row houses was enormous to a girl running. But we never went out of these bounds, even when we reached the end of the boundaries and a boy was right behind us. The street was long and at each end it was bounded by another street and we never crossed those streets. We never went past the two back ways on to streets parallel to our own and we never went into foreign back ways not behind our own houses. In this neighborhood everyone had their block and you didn't leave your block. Our block was white and Jewish. The block across the street on one end of our street was Polish Catholic. The block across the street at the other end of our street was black. Even when we played witch, no matter how hard you wanted to run and get away, you never left the block.

*

I would play witch, racing heart.

*

I would play witch, wanting to be chased and caught, terrified to be chased and caught, terrified not to be chased: racing heart.

*

I would play witch, running, racing heart: running very fast, running away, someone chasing: realizing: you have to slow down to get caught: wanting to be caught: not slowing down.

*

I would play witch, already slow, barely chased, out of breath, hiding, then wander back to where we had started, then wander back to where the wooden cage was and see the girl hoisted in the wooden cage, see the clothesline or rope tied to something and the boys standing there looking up, hear the shrieking.

12

Downhearted, I would wait until they let her down. All the girls would stand around, looking up, looking down, waiting, trying to see who it was, trying to figure out who was missing, who got caught, who was pretty, who slowed down.

*

Inside mother was dying and outside, oh, it was incredible to run, to run, racing heart, around the houses and between the cars and through the alleys and into the half-open garages and just up to the boundaries of the block, farther, farther than you had ever been before, right up to the edge: to run with a boy chasing you and then to saunter on alone, out of breath, having run and run and run. If only that had been the game. But the game was to get caught and put in the cage and hoisted up the telephone pole, tied by rope. Sometimes they would tie your hands behind you and sometimes they would put tape over your mouth. The game was to be the witch and have them chase you and catch you and put you in a wooden cage and tie your hands and hoist you up a telephone pole and tie the rope so the cage would stay up high: you weren't supposed to want to be the witch but if you were a girl and running there was nothing else to want because the game was for the boys to chase you. Everyone else just stood around waiting until the boys got bored and tired and let the witch down.

*

The horses were running as fast as they could, Roy Rogers was sort of standing up on the wagon driving them on, shouting go boy go faster faster, and you could see the horses streaking by up and down the roughest mountain roads, the fringes on his cowboy jacket were all swept back by the wind, and he looked back over his shoulder as he sort of stood up and shook the reins so the horses would go faster and shouted how you doing back there do you like this you uppity little thing or something like that with his grin from ear to ear like a smartass, and instead of the covered part of a covered wagon there was a wooden cage like maybe from a medicine show that had a circus and transported animals and it was heaving over the rough roads at the full speed of the horses with Roy making them go faster and faster and up against the slats Dale Evans was holding on, her face all dirty, imprisoned in the wooden cage and saying she would never speak to him and he had

13

better let her go. She had been snotty to him and he had gotten her in the cage and locked her in and taken off, making the horses go faster and faster and she was screaming and screaming for him to stop and saying she never would never not as long as she lived and he was shouting back over his shoulder as the hills flashed by and the horses' manes stood up on end from the wind and the fringe on his cowboy jacket went the same direction as the horses' manes and his gun and holster were tied to his leg, had enough yet I'll tame you you little devil. Eventually she was tired and dirty and saw he was stronger and she got quiet and loved him and he won. They were in love then. Once she quieted down he slowed down the horses and took her back to town, leaving her in the cage, singing her a song. Back in town, all his friends, the Sons of the Pioneers, got to see her come out of the cage, quiet, dirty, and she got out of the cage, all the men knowing.

*

I had a cowgirl suit, a cowgirl hat, a gun, a holster. There was nothing more important than being a cowboy, even though I had to be a cowgirl because I had to wear a skirt, with fringes, and a blouse, with fringes, and the cowgirl hat and the gun and holster didn't entirely make up for it. It was my favorite thing to wear, even though we never did play cowboys and Indians. It had more to do with wanting to be a gunslinger and learning how to draw fast and shoot straight. I would practice my draw for hours at a time but no one would go along with me and have a gunfight. I would draw my gun on my father and my brother, who would be wrestling and tickling on the living room floor. There was vague disapproval of the gun in the air and so I would shoot it outside and it would make a huge noise and I would gleefully shoot round after round of caps, a red paper that sort of exploded and burned. I had a rifle too and boots. But it was the gun I loved, and Annie Oakley. She wore a skirt and was a crack shot and once we went to see her at a live show with Gene Autry. I wanted to be her or Roy Rogers or the Lone Ranger, not Dale Evans, not ever, not as long as I lived.

*

The wooden cage would hang from the telephone pole, hoisted by a rope or a piece of clothesline. It would dangle there, the

14

girl inside it not easy to see. They would push her around before they put her in the cage. Sometimes they would tie her hands. The wooden cage hung over the black asphalt lined by garages, some open, some not, and garbage cans, all the fathers at work, all the mothers inside the houses or in the front on the steps visiting. It would be desolate on the asphalt, boys all huddled around the cage with the one caught girl, and slowly girls converging back there from all the directions they had run in, some coming back from a long way away, having run and hidden, run to the very edges of the boundaries of our street or having run up and down the back ways and in and out of garages, avoiding boys, hiding from them, and then enough time would pass, and they would dare to drift back, lonely perhaps, thinking enough time had gone by that someone else had been caught or the game was over, and there would always be the one girl surrounded by boys being pushed into the cage and the cage being hoisted off the ground, or the cage would already be tied up there. And the boys would stand under it, watching it, watching her, and the other girls would stay far away, around the edges, each alone, afraid to get too close, afraid perhaps that the boys would grab them and do something to them, also lonely, also left out. It was our saddest game. It never ended right.

*

It would begin in a blaze of excitement. Someone would say let's play witch. Everyone's eyes would look wildly around, scanning the street for where the adults were. We were accomplices in this game. We all knew not to tell. No one ever talked about this game or mentioned it any other time than when we were going to play. The boys would get together and count to ten fast because it was a ferocious game: the chase was fierce and fast and it had to be close and there had to be the excitement of being almost caught or having a hard time getting away and they had to be able to see you and get you. It wasn't a patient game like hide-and-seek. It was a feverish game, and it would begin at a fever pitch of the boys chasing and you running as hard and as fast as you could but you wanted to keep them after you as much as you didn't want to be caught so you would have to slow down to stay in sight, and they would divide up going in twos and threes after one girl or another and they would hunt someone down but if she wasn't the one they wanted they would pretend not to see her finally hiding or they would suddenly turn and run after someone else or run in another direction pretending to run after someone else and in the end they would all have circled the same girl, whoever they had decided on, and they would herd her from wherever they had caught her, sometimes far away from the wooden cage, and push her and shove her until they got her to the telephone pole with the wooden cage. Once they caught her it was against the rules for her not to go with them anyway. The game slowed down after the first few minutes and each girl was running on her own figuring out, independent of what the boys had planned, whether she wanted to be caught or not: and what to do to get caught or not to get caught: and did the boys want her anyway? It became a game of slow loneliness, of staggering solitude: breathless, dizzy, she would stop running in a fever and turn to see no one chasing, no one following. Had she won, outsmarted them, outrun them, or had she lost, they had never really been after her anyway. She might hide, or stalk the boys, dazzle them by showing herself, and then they would chase her and she would lose them again or hadn't they really tried at all? Or she would see one in the distance, maybe half a block away, and he didn't see her, or did he, and she would start running and running and congratulate herself on getting away, or had she? Then a long time would go by and she would get bored and tired and want the game to be over and wonder where everybody was and make her way back to the starting point and no one would be there so she would make her way to the back alley and the telephone pole, but from far away, toward it but not to it, not directly walk up to it, always stay far away from it and the boys, safe, and see the boys huddling around the cage and try to see who was in it and hear the screams and watch the cage go up, two or three boys hoisting it while the rest stood under it and watched, and you could never see who it was. Later when they let her down you could see. They would untie her hands and walk away and she would be left there and the scattered ring of lonely girls would watch. She was the witch. No one talked to her at least the rest of the day.

*

The convent gave us the right atmosphere. We never saw anything except the thick stone walls, and they were thick, not brick or cement, but huge stones like something medieval, black and dark gray with moss and other hanging things and shadows falling like God over the stones: and above the high walls thick leafy green trees all casting shadows and it seemed like no sky or light could ever get through them, in or out. It was completely silent. We never saw anything or heard anything. No door ever opened or closed. No Latin poured out, no bells chimed, no music pierced the early dawn or night. The wooden cage was hoisted in the back alley closest to the convent, and you could see it from there, hanging over the tops of the houses, a place of gothic mystery, Catholic, eerie. From the telephone pole, hoisted up, inside the wooden cage, you were raised above the stone walls and the ghastly trees: and with your hands tied there you were the witch: and the Catholics could see you.

They had things called nuns, women dressed all in black, all covered up, and we thought they walked around in twos and never said a word and had their heads bowed and shaved and their hands together in prayer. But we didn't know. We weren't supposed to go too near it, the convent, and we were afraid of disappearing in there for life, because once you went in you could never come out. There were ghosts there too. We didn't know if anyone in there was really alive. When you saw the top of the convent and the menacing trees above the backs of the row houses and the wooden cage with a slight figure inside it hoisted high on the telephone pole and tied there with a rope and the afternoon began to fade and it got dusky or cloudy and there were just the silhouettes of things, the starkness of the cage and the figure in it, the tautness of the rope, the city ugliness, barren, of the telephone pole, all against a sky that had begun to lose light, reigned over by old European stones and impenetrable trees, you knew you were near something old, chill, something you knew but didn't know: something God was supposed to protect you from: something on the edge of your memory, but not your memory. When it got late in the day or the sky darkened with clouds or oncoming rain, the silhouettes were awful drawings of something you had seen before: maybe in a book: somewhere: and you stood completely still and watched and prayed for the wooden cage to come down, for the figure in it to disappear, not be there, that slight figure, for the convent to go away, to be somewhere else: and especially for the dread boys, the crowd, to notice the coming dark and be afraid of what they had done. We were overcome watching: the great shadow of the convent and its thick trees, its cold walls of stone, and the great imposition of the wooden cage and the caged figure on the darkening sky. It was eerie and unhappy: and one was drawn and repelled: drawn to the convent and the cage, wanting to run inside the house.

We were all supposed to stay away from Catholics. The convent represented their strangeness and malice: the threat of their ghostly superstitions. A holy ghost lived there and they drank blood and ate cookies and kneeled down. They wanted all the children: and at night you could disappear into those walls and no one would ever see you again. Standing outside the great stone thing, even in broad daylight, even with traffic all around, because one side of the convent was right on a very big street at a very big intersection, a child was frightened of the unscalable cold stone and the height of it. We could never find a way in or out and the walls were too high to climb. I wanted to see it and go into it but I was afraid even to stand near it. Once another girl and I stood on that street corner for hours collecting money for a charity and if you got enough money you got to go to a special dinner in a restaurant and I just thought about the traffic, how regular it was, and the sun, how bright it was, the people walking on the street, how they looked and dressed, because behind me was the penetrating silence of those stone walls and I was cold and afraid. I could feel it behind my back and I could feel the cold stones there and I could feel the giant height of the wall and I could feel the reaching coolness of the shadows from the great trees. Then a car stopped to give us money after we had been there for hours and this girl I was with went up to the car and then she got real frightened and wouldn't say what the man said to her and said we had to go home right away and was really scared and since it was right next to the convent I knew it was something really bad so we went right home and she talked to her mother who talked to my mother and I kept asking what had happened and what the man had done to her. Finally my mother said he asked her to get in the car with him. It was very terrible and ominous to get into the car. The air was heavy with warning and fear and my own inestimable incomprehension. There was this edging of my fear away from the convent to the man in the car and to getting into a car. I thought he must be Catholic. The girl would never speak of it or answer anything I asked. My mother said never to say anything about it. I asked if he had hurt her. My mother said: he didn't get the chance.

*

There were Jewish blocks and Catholic blocks and black blocks. We were supposed to stay off the black blocks, though it was never put that way. We were always just showed how to walk, down which streets, and told where not to go, which streets. The streets we weren't supposed to go on just had that in common: black faces, black children. The Catholic streets and the Jewish streets were all inside the same area, alternating, no mixing. But I liked to go where I wasn't supposed to, and I often walked home alone down the Catholic streets, because no one could tell by just looking at me exactly. I would make new routes for myself down streets my friends didn't go on. Sometimes I went down black streets, because I wanted to. Then, getting closer to the one central elementary school, where all kinds of children converged from every direction, there were blocks that we all had to walk down because we were all going to the same place and it was just a fact that no matter who lived there we all had to walk by or through, however timidly.

Our street was bounded on one end, the one going to school, by a busy street with lots of cars and across that street was a Catholic block, Polish. We were supposed to walk up half a block before crossing that busy street and continue going toward school on a Jewish block, and usually I did. But coming home I would want to walk down the Catholic block because it was different and it seemed more direct. I knew I shouldn't but I didn't exactly know why I shouldn't except that it did seep in that they were different from us and we weren't supposed to marry them. I wasn't even ten yet because I was ten when we moved away.

I had a friend on that block, Joe, and we would say hello and talk and say shy things to each other. Their houses were different, all brick row houses, but right on the sidewalks, no flights of steps going up to the door, just one level block. There were more gardens. Kids didn't stay outside playing that I could see. Or maybe there weren't any, I don't know. Joe had grease on his hair and it was combed very straight and sticky sort of, and he wore checkered shirts, and he talked different but I don't know why or how: he didn't seem to be used to talking. He was a teenager. I would walk down the street and he would sort of come out and I wouldn't know what to say, except one day I smiled and he said hello, and then after that I would decide if I was going to walk down the Catholic block or not and if I was chasing boys and what was wrong with him that I wasn't supposed to talk with him and I couldn't talk with him too long or someone would notice that I hadn't come home with my friends on my block. And I used to come home other ways too, where I had no one to talk to. I would walk home by the convent and try to hear things inside it, and sometimes I would walk home on the black blocks, all alone. This was my secret life.

*

There was an alley next to a church on the way to school and we would always try to get lost in it. It was only a tiny alley, very narrow but long, dark and dusty, with stray cats and discarded bottles and strange trash and urine and so even children knew its every creak and crevice very soon. But we would close our eyes and spin each other around and do everything we could not to know how to get out. We would spend hours pretending to be lost. We would try to get into the church but it was always closed. We would play adventures in which someone was captured and lost in the alley and someone else had to get her out. But mostly we would flail around being lost, the worst thing being that we would know exactly where we were and there were no adventures and we couldn't go in the church. Then sometimes suddenly we would really be lost and we would try to find our way out and not be able to no matter how hard we tried and it would start getting dark and we would get scared and somehow when we got scared enough we would remember how to get out of the alley and how to get home.

*

We had to walk a long way to and from school, four times a day: to school, home for lunch, back to school, home at the end of school; or sometimes we had to go to the Hebrew School after school, twice a week. In school all the children were together, especially the Polish Catholics and the blacks and the Jews, and after school we didn't speak to each other or be friends. I would try to go to the houses of kids I liked in school, just walk by to see what it was like if it was near where I walked to go home, and there would be polite conversations sometimes on their blocks, but their parents would look at me funny and I could never go in. We got to love each other in school and play together at recess but then no more, we had to go back to where we came from. We had to like each other on our block whether we did or not and it was OK when we were playing massive games ranging over the whole wide world of our block, but sometimes when I just wanted to talk to someone or see someone, one person, it wasn't someone on our block, but someone else, someone Polish Catholic or black, and then I couldn't: because it just couldn't be done, it just wasn't allowed. My parents were good, they were outspoken against prejudice and they taught me everybody was the same, but when it came to actually going on another block they just said not to go there and there and there like everybody else and when I tried to go there the parents on the other end would send me away. There was Michael who was Polish Catholic, a gentle boy, and Nat who was black. She would come to my house and once at least I went to hers, at least once or twice I was allowed to go there, mostly she came home with me, my parents protected me and didn't let me know how the neighbors felt about it, and we always had to stay inside and play, and her mother was a teacher and so was my father: and I loved her with all my passionate heart. When we moved away to the suburbs so mother wouldn't have to walk any steps because she couldn't breathe I was torn apart from all this, my home, my street, the games, the great throng of wild children who played hide-and-seek late into the night while mother lay dying: and I said, I will go if I can see Nat, if she can come to visit me and I can visit her, and I was so distressed and full of grief, that they looked funny at each other and lied and said yes of course you can see Nat.

But where we moved was all white and I couldn't see Nat.

*

So when I was a teenager I went back to the old neighborhood to show it to a teenage friend, the old elementary school where I had been happy and the old streets where I had been happy, we took two buses to get there and walked a long way and I didn't tell anyone I was going, but now it was all black and getting even poorer than it had been and there were hundreds of teenage girls in great clusters on the streets walking home from high school and we were white and we were surrounded and they got nasty and mean and wanted to know why we were showing our white faces there and I looked up and there was Nat, quiet as she had always been, the same scholarly serious face and long braids, now teenage like me, and black, and with a gang of girls, and she told them to leave me alone and so they did and she walked away with them looking away from me, looking grave and sad and even a little confused: walking away from me, but I was the deserter. I watched her walking away, and I still see the look on her face even with my eyes open, a remorseless understanding of something I didn't know but she did and whatever it was I had found her but it didn't matter because of whatever it was. It was the saddest moment of my life. Later, mother died. I didn't laugh or weep or understand. Why are they gone?

Neither weep nor laugh but understand.
Spinoza

*

Mother would be sick and dad worked two jobs, teaching and in the post office unloading packages. Mother would be upstairs in her bedroom in bed, near death, or in the hospital, near death. My brother would be sent somewhere and I would be sent somewhere: to separate relatives, suddenly, in the middle of the night. But sometimes we were allowed to stay home. A black girl would put us in the bath together and wash us and put us to bed. My brother and I would play and splash water and the black girl would wash us and smile, but she was always tentative, never belonging there. She was always young, there were so many, even I knew she was young, not as old as any other big people I had ever seen, and for days on end she would be the only one to talk to us or touch us or do anything with us. They were nice to us but never said much and none stayed too long because we were too poor to pay for help and eventually we always had to be farmed out separately to one relative or another. The house of our parents would be dank with disease and despair, my father's frenetic dinner served so fast because he had to get to his second job, the only minutes we could even see him or hear his voice, and the only one who talked to us or was nice to us was the black girl who put us in the bath together where we played and played, after we had our argument about who had to sit on the end with the faucet, and she put us to bed: and I always wanted her to stay and be my friend or at least talk and say things I could understand like other people did. No one stayed long enough so that I remember her name because we were funny kinds of orphans: mother wasn't dead but dying; father loved us but couldn't be there; the relatives split us up so we were always alone in strange houses surrounded by strange ways of doing things and adults who weren't as nice to us as our father was and they thought that if they were your grandmother or aunt it made being there less lonely: which it did not. They must have been teenagers, so much bigger than we were that they seemed

23

like adults. They must have been poorer than even we were. They were black and we were white: and whoever it is I remember, on your knees by the bathtub, as the blond-haired baby boy and I splashed and squealed, as you dabbed and rubbed, whoever it is: where are you now? and why were you there at all? and why couldn't you stay? and while mother lay dying, you were kind.

*

Once mother was hiring the girl herself. She must have been a little better then, standing up in the living room, dressed in regular clothes not sick clothes, without my father there or any doctor. I came in and there were lots of women and my mother talked to them one at a time but all in the same room and one was white and the rest were black and my mother said who would you like to have and I said hire the white one.

*

I had never seen a white one so I said hire the white one.

*

Hire the white one, I said, maybe seven years old. Hire the white one. My dying mother hit me.

*

When we had to move from Camden because my mother couldn't walk steps or breathe and was frail and dying, the neighbors on our block got sullen and banded together and came and said don't you sell to blacks. Our next-door neighbor got sullen and threatening and said don't you sell to blacks. These are our friends, said my parents. We will do what's right, don't you worry, said my father ambiguously. We sold to Polish Catholics, blond, with heavy foreign accents. Not Jews but not black. The best offer, my father swore. The neighbors were chilly anyway but soon they all moved. The blacks were coming closer. So they sold to blacks and moved out.

*

One of the houses where I had to stay was my uncle's: marriage, not blood. He was richer than us, a judge, a reform democratic politician even though he had friends in the Klan, and he was vulgar, and I hated him, and the reform democrats won and my uncle and his friends looted the city and got rich and that's why the blacks in Camden are so poor.

I would be delivered to his house and his cronies would come and they would talk about the niggers and even when they were the government of the city they were planning to move out to somewhere else and they planned to steal especially from the school system, or that was the part I heard: they stole equipment from Head Start programs and looted school equipment and cheated on school-lunch programs and left the blacks to die and called them niggers and my uncle had a bar where he sold the niggers liquor and ridiculed them for getting drunk and bragged that he could sell them horseshit and they would drink it. He had friends who were friends of Nixon and friends who were friends of the Klan. Now Camden is a ghost town with black ghosts on those streets where we played our real childhood games. I had a divine childhood, even with the woman dying, and father away day and night working, and death coming suddenly, and my brother and me separated over and over, orphans in different places for years at a time: I ran in those streets and played hide-and-seek and Red Rover Red Rover and jumped rope and played fish and washed my doll's hair with the other girls outside on the steps and sat behind cars near telephone poles and on strange days played witch: it was divine until I was torn away from it: and I walked down Catholic streets and black streets without anyone knowing and I loved Joe and Nat and Michael: then the vultures moved in when I had gone away, but I heard their plans and I know what they did: and the wonderful neighbors on the block where I lived hated blacks: and I said hire the white one at seven years old: and the vultures picked the bones of the city and left it plundered. Oh, Nat, where are you? Did you weep or laugh or understand?

Neither weep nor laugh but understand.

Spinoza

*

We were very tiny, in the third grade—how small are seven-
and eight-year-olds?—the little girls from my block. We were
on a big street not too far from the school, one you had to
walk down. It was a rich street, completely different from ours.
There was no brick. There were big windows in the fronts of
the houses and each one had a different front, some rounded
or curved. There were fences around the few very nice steps up
to the door, ornamentation on the outside, around the
windows or on the façade, wide sidewalks, huge trees lining
the street so it was always shady even in the early afternoon
when we went home from school. We were small and happy,
carrying our books home, chattering away. A bunch of black
girls approached us, surrounded us. They were twice as tall as
we were, real big, from junior high school. They surrounded
us and began teasing and calling us names. They demanded
Diane's scarf. We were silent, very afraid. She was beginning
to give them the scarf when I said no, don't. There was one
minute of stunned silence, then raucous laughter: wha you say
girl? Don't, don't give it to them. Now why not girl we gonna
take it anyway. Because stealing is wrong, I said sincerely. They
surrounded me and began beating me, punching me, kicking
me. They kept on punching and kicking. I remember falling
and saliva pouring from my mouth and screaming. They kept
punching me in the stomach until I fell all the way to the
ground then they kicked me in the stomach over and over and
then they ran away. I lay on the ground quite a while. No one
offered to help me up. Everyone just stared at me. I got up but
I couldn't get all the way up because I couldn't straighten my
stomach, it hurt too much. I held it with both hands and stood
bent-backed. No one touched me or helped me or spoke to
me. I must have said something like my daddy told me it's not
right to steal. Then someone said that she knew someone who
said my daddy was a sissy. A what? A sissy. He's a sissy. What
does that mean, I must have asked. You know, she said, that's

26

what all the boys say, that he's a sissy. Enraged, I walked doubled up home, determined to find the girls who had beat me up. But my parents told me not to because they would just hurt me more. I wanted to go into every junior high school class and look for them. But it would just make trouble and they would hurt me more, I was told. I remembered *sissy* and I remembered my girlfriends doing nothing. They were somehow worse than awful and mean. Doing nothing was worse.

*

When you get beat up you don't see much, you begin falling, you begin trying not to fall so you feel yourself falling and you feel yourself trying to stay straight and the fists come from every direction, down on your head and in your face and in your gut most, and you keep not falling until you can't breathe anymore and then you fall. You hit the cement and you feel it hit you and you see the feet coming at you and you keep trying to protect your face especially and your eyes and your teeth and if you can move once you're down you try to kick back, to use your legs to get them off of you, but if you fall so that your legs are sort of twisted under you then you can't do that and you can feel your back twist away from your stomach and it's real hard not to piss and once they've stopped it's real hard not to vomit. You don't know anything about other people except the ones hitting you if there are a mess of them and they are all punching you at once. You don't think, oh, my friends are standing around watching. It's after, when you are suddenly alone, when the heat of the hitting bodies is suddenly cold air on your sweat and you suddenly understand that you are not being punched anymore, it has stopped, and you are not being kicked anymore, it has stopped, and you think, oh, I'm not dead, I can breathe, now let's see if I can move, and you try to stand up no matter what it costs because standing is the best thing, it gives you something back, and it is in the process of trying to get up that you look around and see your friends watching, and it is in the process of getting up that you see you have to do it alone, and it is in the process of getting up that you realize without even thinking that anyone can see how much you hurt and your friends are just standing there, watching, staying away from you. It is the process of getting up that clarifies for you how afraid they were for themselves, not for you, and how chickenshit they are, and even though you are tiny and they are tiny you know that even tiny little girls aren't really that tiny, in fact no one on earth is that tiny, and then they say *sissy* and it makes you understand that you and your daddy are different from them *forever* and there is something puny at the heart of them that smells up the sky. You can be seven or eight and know all that and remember it forever.

*

Diane was holding her scarf, real pretty with lots of very pretty colors: and it was Marcy who said, your daddy is a sissy.

*

I got home down long blocks bent over and not crying and they walked all around me not touching me, staying far away. My stomach was kicked in but my face wasn't hurt too bad. I was bent and there was no way on earth I could straighten out my back or straighten out my stomach or take my hands away from my stomach but see I kept walking and they kept walking: oh, and after that everything was the same, except I never really liked Marcy again, as long as I live I never will: and I still would have done anything for Diane: and we played outside all our games: and I didn't care whether they lived or died.

*

Down the far end of our block, not the end going toward school but the end going somewhere I never saw, there was a real funny girl, H. She lived almost at the very end of our block, it was like almost falling off the edge of the world to go there and you had to pass by so many people you knew to get there and they expected you not to go that far away from where you lived, from the center of the block, and they wondered where you were going and what you were going to do, and I didn't know too many people up that end, just some, not any of my favorites: and also the principal of the Hebrew School was up that way, and I didn't like going by his house at all because in heavy European tones he chastised me for being alive and skipping about with no apparent purpose. So I avoided going there at all, and also I was really scared to be so close to the end of the block, but this girl was really funny and so sometimes I went there anyway. She had a real nice mother

28

and a sort of bratty younger brother. It was the same basic house as ours but with lots more things in it, lots nicer: and her mother was always cheerful and upright and never up dying in bed, which was as pleasant as anything could be. We weren't real close friends but there was some wild streak that matched: she had it by being real funny, crazy funny, and I had it some other way, I don't know how I had it or how she knew I had it, but she always liked me so she must have.

One regular Saturday afternoon H's mother went away and her father was working and she and her bratty brother were being baby-sitted and I went there to visit. The baby-sitter was some gray gray teenager with pimples and a ponytail, and we just got wilder and wilder until we ended up on top of her holding her down and punching her and hitting her and taunting her and tormenting her and calling her names and telling her how ugly she was: and then the bratty brother came down and we got scared for a minute that he was going to tell or she was going to get up because we were getting pretty tired but he came right over and sat right on top of her and we kept hitting her and laughing like mad and having so much fun making jokes about hitting her and calling her names and then making jokes about that. H was at her head holding her down by pulling her hair and sitting on her hair and slapping her in the face and hitting her breasts. The bratty brother was sitting sort of over her stomach and kept hitting her there and tickling her there and grinding his knees into her sides. I was at her feet, sitting on top of them and digging my nails into her legs and punching her legs and hitting her between her legs. We kept her there for hours, at least two, and we never stopped laughing at our jokes and at how stupid and pathetic she was: and when we let her up she ran out and left us: and when H's mother came home we said the baby-sitter had just left us there to go see her boyfriend: and H's mother was furious with the baby-sitter for leaving us alone because we were just children and she called to complain and call her down and got some hysterical story of how we had tortured her: and we said, what does that mean? what is that? what is torture? she left to see her boyfriend, that's what she said to us: and the baby-sitter said we beat her up and tortured her and we said no no we don't know what she means: and no one ever believed her. She wasn't Jewish was the thing. It was incredible fun was the thing. She was dumber and weaker than we were was the thing. Especially: it was incredible fun was the thing. I never laughed so much in my life. She wept but I'm sure she didn't understand. You can't feel remorse later when you laughed so hard then. I have never—to this day and including right now—given a damn. Why is it that when you laugh so hard you can't weep or understand? Oh, little girls, weep forever or understand too much but be a little scared to laugh too hard.

Neither weep nor laugh but understand.

Spinoza

*

There was a stone fence, only about two feet high, uneven, rough, broken, and behind it the mountains: a hill declining, rolling down, and beyond the valley where it met the road the mountains rose up, not hills but high mountain peaks, in winter covered in snow from top to bottom, in fall and spring the peaks white and blindingly bright and the rest underneath the pearly caps browns and greens and sometimes dark, fervent purples where the soil mixed with varying shades of light coming down from the sky. The building near the stone wall, facing out in back over the descending hill to the road and then the grandeur of the mountains, was white and wood, old, fragile against this bold scenery, slight against it. When it snowed the frail building could have been part of a drawing, a mediocre, sentimental New England house in a New England snow, a white on white cliché, except exquisite: delicate, exquisite, so finely drawn under its appearance of being a cheap scene of the already observed, the clichéd, the worn-down-into-the-ground snow scene. In the fall, the trees were lush with yellow and crimson and purple saturated the distant soil. Green got duller, then turned a burnt brown. The sky was huge, not sheltering, but right down on the ground with you so that you walked in it: your feet had to reach down to touch earth. Wind married the sky and tormented it: but the earth stayed below solid and never swirled around in the fight. There was no dust. The earth was solid down in the ground, always. There was no hint of impermanence, sand. This was New England, where the ground did not bend or break or compromise: it rested there, solid and placid and insensitive to the forms its own magnificence took as it rose up in mountains of ominous heights. These were not mountains that crumbled or fell down in manic disorder. These were not mountains that slid or split apart or foamed over. These were mountains where the sky reached down to touch them in their solid splendor with their great trees and broken branches and dwarfed stones, and they

31

stayed put because the earth was solid, just purely itself, not mixed with sky or air or water, not harboring fire or ash: no ice sliding down to kill anything in its path: no snow tumbling to destroy: just dirt, solid ground, made so that humans could comprehend it, not die in awe of it, while snow packed itself down on top or rain pelted or punched or sun burnt itself out or wind flashed through the sky, torturing it. These were mountains meant to last forever in a community of human sight and sound: not mountains meant to swallow cities and towns forever: and so one was surrounded by a beauty not suffused with fear, splendid but not inducing awe of the divine or terror of the wild, intemperate menace of weather and wind gone amuck. These were mountains that made humans part of their beauty: solid, like earth, like soil. One felt immeasurably human, solid, safe: part of the ground, not some shade on it through which the wind passes. The mountains could be one's personal legacy, what the earth itself gave one to be part of: one simply had to love them: nothing had to be done to deserve them or survive them: one could be innocent of nature and not offend them.

The wooden house, so white and old, underlined the tameness of these mountains, the incongruity fitting right in, a harmony, a simple delight. The mountains and the house went hand in hand: what would the mountain be without the simple old house? The cold came from the sky and rested on the ground: touched the edges of the mountains high up and reached down into the valley and edged along the road and paced restlessly on the earnest ground. The cold could overwhelm a human with its intensity, its bitterness, like some awful taste rubbing on the skin. But in the fragile wooden house it was warm: so the cold was not the terrifying cold that could penetrate even stone or brick: this must be a gentle cold, killed by small fires in charming fireplaces and rattling radiators in tiny rooms.

Emmy and I never touched, outsiders at this rich girls' school, on this campus nestled in these welcoming mountains: she from Kenya, me from Camden; her an orphan separated from her family to be sent to a girls' school in New England as a little girl; me with the woman upstairs dying and the father gone to work and the brother farmed out and me farmed out, poor little poor girl; her angry and wild, dark black, separated from everyone she loved and everyone she knew and arriving here at this college after three or four finishing schools, unfinished, to be educated; me having gotten here so I could read and write; her wanting to go home; me never having a home anymore again; her not a rich white girl here at this right school; me poor; her upper-class where she comes from; me low down; both smart, too smart, for our own good. Also: in the world of the rich the poor are outcasts. Being black made her poor, money aside. The others were like some distant figures who spoke with cotton stuffed in their mouths: nothing ever came out clean and clear; they had anguish but it was fogged, having nothing to do with what she or I understood as real: not that any of the premises were discussed, because the rich make their own rules, democracy being one of them, the democracy being in the pretense that no rules have been made: they suspend them at will: they don't know: it's not their fault. She had a country to think about and plan for: the freedom of its people and her place there, now that she had been "educated," westernized, Europeanized: she knew it but not what to do about it, and however happy we were, in her head she was always on her way home, to a place where she would still be an outsider, in exile from a youth that had been stolen from her. I loved her. I never touched her.

*

The color that comes to New England in the fall does not leave it when the trees die. Winter is not barren or monotone. The great evergreens go on in muted light. The bare branches themselves are tinted with purples and yellows and tawny shades like deer flashing by at incredible speeds. The ground is every color of brown and blue and black with yellow and red running through it like great streaks, and the purple lies in the ground like some spectral presence waiting to rise up. The air is silver and blue as it edges toward black. It has the purest white and the grim gray of a sober storm and in the center of it will hang the most orange sun, flaming like dreaded fire. In the fall there are only dizzying spreads of scarlet and yellow or crimson and ochre: but in the winter, the colors are endlessly subtle and complex: so many shades of brown that they cannot be counted or named, so much purple in the air between the

33

trees and under the earth shining through and sliding down the mountainsides that when the yellow seeps in or crowds in next to the purple the mind renounces what it sees, saying: impossible, winter is something brown and dead. The branches of the trees are elegant, so strong and graceful, even under the weight of icy snows: the ice rides them like the best lover, an unsentimental kindness of enveloping, hugging, holding on, no matter what the pressure is to shake loose. The white branches stand in solemn quietude, witnesses without speech to the death called winter, reproaches to the effrontery of other seasons with their vulgar displays. The white on the mountains reaches out to the human eye, persuading it that winter is entirely sublime and will stay forever, also persuading the human heart that nothing is beyond it—no cold too cold, no snow too big, no winter too long, no death entirely bereft of some too simple beauty, no tree too bare, no color too insignificant or too subtle, no silence too still, no gesture too eloquent, no human act merely human. In these winter mountains, the human heart learns to want peace.

The trees near the fragile white house are endlessly high. They disappear into some low-hanging cloud, all white and puffy, wispy, watery, dripping ice that melts and burns in the bright sun before it gets down to the ground. They are great carcasses rooted in the solid ground, great thick things all knotted and gnarled, or smooth and silver-streaked. They never were just leaves: the bright colors deceived the stupid mind. They were always their trunks, with great canals going through them and animals living inside. They have other things growing on them, even in the dead of winter, even partly buried under the snow or whiplashed by it as the snow swipes on by carried by the wind in a storm. The great trunks deceive us into seeing them all white in a snowstorm: but they always stay themselves, the misery-racked survivors of every assault and intrusion, every wind and falling thing, every particle blown by or falling down, every stone or rock hurled against them or brushing by: the trunk is immoveable while everything else, except the ground underneath, moves or dies. This is a permanence beyond our own, redeemed by having no memory and no human speech.

Emmy had come from a place entirely unlike this and so

had I. She said almost nothing about hers, except that there was a huge city, cosmopolitan, exciting, and a university, big, important, and all around the lush, infested green of hot jungle thick with insects and heat. It had many languages, tribal and colonial. It was troubling somehow: because there might not be room for her there. Mine was simpler, city, a suburb later on briefly: telephone poles, asphalt, seasons, the ubiquitous cement, the endless chatter of automobiles and human talk: not the grandeur of mountains. She hadn't seen snow, except maybe once before she came here. For me snow had been: trying to get back and forth from school with the boys surrounding the girls, chasing us, heading us off, pelting us with snowballs, and the snow melting under the dirty car smoke and turning brown and greasy, and a shovel to dig out the cars and clear the sidewalks, and playing in the snow dressed in snowsuits and trying to make a snowman: but especially, trying to get back and forth from school without getting hurt by a snowball. My snow had nothing to do with solitude or beauty and it fell on a flat place, not a hill or mountain, with the cement under it less solid than this New England earth, less trustworthy, ready to break and split, ready to loosen and turn into jagged pieces of stone big enough to throw instead of snowballs or inside them. We were endlessly strange together, not rich, foreign to this cool, elegant, simple, beautiful winter.

I didn't touch her, but I touched him. Her best friend since childhood, both in Kenya, little kids together and now here, preparing, preparing for some adult future back home. She took me with her and delivered me to him and I took him instead of her, because he was as close as I could get. She was delighted he liked me, and sullen. It happened in a beautiful room, an elegant room, at elegant Harvard, friends of theirs from home, their room, all students studying to be the future of their country, and I was bleeding anyway and so I spread my legs for him, not knowing of course that it was because I loved her. I stayed with him over and over, for months, a night here, an afternoon there, though I came to hate him, a purely physical aversion to his clumsy, boring fuck: I didn't want him to touch me but I had him fuck me anyway, too polite to say no for one thing, not knowing how to get out of it, and wanting her, not knowing it. I got pregnant and had an abortion and she went home. Nothing like pregnancy to make the man disappear. It decided her. The years of exiled youth ended. She went home. Like everyone else in the world I was terrified, it would have been easier right then to be an outcast hero and have a little black baby whom I could love to death without having to say why and I would have felt brave, brave: and no one would have hurt that child: but Emmy looked at me a certain way all the time now, hate, simple, pure, and I had the abortion, the hate was hard as a rock, diamond, shredding the light. She got so quiet I could have died. She left, but I was the deserter. I didn't care too much. By the time mother died everyone was a stranger anyway, and after that I was a too-cold child with a too-cold heart. I have stayed that way. Everything gets taken away and everyone eventually weeps and laughs and understands. Why lie?

> The great thing is to be *saturated* with
> something—that is, in one way or another,
> with life; and I chose the form of my
> saturation.
>
> Henry James

*

Have you ever seen the Lower East Side of New York in the summer? The sidewalks are boiling cement, almost molten, steaming, a spread of heat scorching human feet, the heat like the pure blue of the pure flame, pure heat saddled with city dirt and city smell and especially the old urine of the hundreds of near-dead junkies hanging nearly skeletal in the shadows of doorways and crouched under the stinking stairwells of tenements in which the hot, dead air never moves.

The sun burns. It burns like in Africa. It is in the center of the sky, huge and burning. No clouds can cover it. It comes through them, a haze of heat. It gets bigger every day. It is a foul yellow fire, sulfur at the edges. It hangs and burns. It spreads out. It reaches down like the giant hand of some monster. The buildings burn.

The air is saturated with the hot sun, thick with it. The air is a fog of fire and steam. The lungs burn and sweat. The skin drowns in its own boiling water, erupting. The air lies still, layers of itself, all in place like the bodies filed in a morgue, corpses grotesquely shelved. Somewhere corpses and rot hang in the air, an old smell in the old air, the air that has never moved off these city streets, the air that has been waiting through the killer winter to burn, to torment, to smother: to burn: the air that has been there year after year, never moving, but burning more and more summer after summer, aged air, old smell: immortal, while humans die.

There is never any wind. There is never a cool breeze. The sun absorbs the wind. The cement absorbs the wind. The wind evaporates between earth and sky. There is never any air to breathe. There is only heat. Rain disappears in the heat, making the air hotter. Rain hangs in the air, in the thick, hot air: bullets of wet heat stopped in motion. Rain gets hot: water boiled that

37

never cools. Rain becomes steam, hanging in midair: it burns inside the nose, singes the hairs in the nose, scorches the throat: leaves scars on the skin. The air gets wetter and hotter and when the rain stops the air is heavier, thicker, harder to breathe. Rain refreshes only the smell, giving it wings.

The smell is blood on piss. The blood coagulates on the cement, then rots. Knives cut and figures track through the blood making burgundy and scarlet footprints. Cats lap up its edges. It never gets scrubbed out. The rain does not wash it away. Dust mixes in with it. Garbage floats on top of it. Candy bar wrappers get stuck in it. Empty, broken hypodermic needles float. It is a sickening smell, fouling up the street, twisting the stomach into knots of despair and revulsion: still, the blood stays there: old blood followed by new: knives especially: sometimes the sharp shots of gunfire: sometimes the exploding shots of gunfire: the acrid smoke hanging above the blood: sometimes the body is there, smeared, alone, red seeping out or bubbling or spurting: sometimes the body is there, the blood comes out hissing with steam, you can see the steam just above the blood running with it, the blood is hot, it hits the pavement, it hisses, hot on hot: sometimes the person moves, walks, runs, staggers, crawls, the blood trailing behind: it stains the cement: flies dance on it in a horrible, pulsating mass: it coagulates: it rots: it stinks: the smell gets old and never dies. Sometimes the next day or the day after people walk through it and track it around step after step until it is just a faint splash of faded, eerie pink: and the smell is on their shoes and they go home: it gets inside, thrown near a pile of clothes or under the bed: it clings to the floor, crawls along it, vile and faint.

There is other blood. Cats and dogs die bleeding, smashed under cars. Rats and mice die bleeding, poison opening up their insides and the blood splattering out. The carcasses decompose. They are thrown in trash cans or kicked in dark corners or swept under parked cars. Chickens are sacrificed in secret religious rites, sometimes cats. Their necks are slashed and they are found, bloodless. The blood has been drained out. There is no trace of it. Children fall and bleed. Their parents beat them. Women bleed inside or sweating on streetcorners. Blood spurts out when junkies shoot up.

The piss sits like a blessing on the neighborhood. It is the holy seal, the sacramental splendid presence, like God omnipresent. The men piss night and day, against the cars, against the buildings, against the steps, against the doors, against the garbage cans, against the cement, against the window ledges and drainpipes and bicycles: against anything standing still: outside or inside: against the walls of foyers and the walls of halls and on the staircases inside buildings and behind the stairwells. Mixed with the smell of the piss is the scent of human shit, deposited in broken-down parks or in foyers or behind stairwells and the casual smell of dog shit, spread everywhere outside, in heaps. The rat shit is hard and dry, huge droppings in infested buildings, the turds almost as big as dog turds, but harder, finer, rounder.

The heat beats down on the piss and shit and the coagulated blood: the heat absorbs the smell and carries it: the heat turns wet on human skin and the smell sinks in: an urban perfume: a cosmopolitan stench: the poor on the Lower East Side of New York.

*

On this block, there is nothing special. It is hot. It stinks. The men congregate in packs on the hot stoops. It is no cooler at night. Inside the crowded tenements it is burning, harder to find air to breathe, so the men live outside, drinking, shooting up, fights break out like brush fires, radios blare in Spanish, knives flash, money changes hands, empty bottles are hurled against walls or steps or cars or into the gutters of the street, broken glass is underfoot, dazzling, destructive: the men go inside to fuck or eat at whim: outside they are young, dramatic, striking, frenetic until the long periods of lethargy set in and one sees the yellow sallowness of the skin, the swollen eyes bloodshot and hazed over, the veins icy blue and used up. "I got me everything," says Juan, my pretty, wired-up lover, junkie snorting cocaine come to fuck while N and R are in the kitchen. He shows up wired. I hesitate. Perhaps she wants him. We are polite this way. "He wants you," N says with her exquisite courtesy, a formal, passionless, gentle courtesy, graceful and courtly, our code, we have seriously beautiful manners. There are no doors but we don't know what they are for anyway. We have one single mattress on the floor where we

39

sleep. He fucks good, Juan, I like him, he keeps his junk to himself, he can't live long, the coke makes him intense, pulsating, deep thrusts, incredible tension in his hips, hard, muscled hips, not usual for a junkie, I can't feel the smack in his body, no languor anywhere, intense crazed coke fucking, intensely devoted fucking for a junkie. N and R walk by, going out. N gives an appreciative look. She smiles her broad grin. I am groaning under him. She laughs her comradely, amused laugh, grinning from ear to ear.

*

The apartment is a storefront. You walk down a few steps to get to the door. Anyone can hide down where you have to walk. The whole front of the apartment is a store window. There is no way to open it. It is level with the street. It has nothing to keep anyone out, no bars, no grating. It is just a solid sheet of glass. The front room is right there, on the street. We keep it empty except for some clothes in our one closet. The middle room is right behind the front room, no door, just a half wall dividing the two rooms. No window. We have one single mattress, old, a sheet or two, a pillow or two, N's record player and her great jazz and blues and classical records, her clarinet, her saxophone, my typewriter, an Olivetti portable, a telephone. Behind the middle room is a large kitchen, no door between the rooms. There is a big wooden table with chairs. There are old, dirty appliances: old refrigerator, old stove. We don't cook much or eat much. We make buckets of iced tea. We have vodka in the refrigerator, sometimes whiskey too. Sometimes we buy orange juice. There are cigarettes on the table, butts piled up in muddy ashtrays or dirty, wet cups. There are some books and some paper and some pencils. There is a door and a window leading out back. The door has heavy metal grating over it, iron, weaved, so that no one can break in. The window is covered in the same heavy metal. The door is bolted with a heavy metal bolt and locked with a heavy metal police lock.

The floors are wooden and painted. The apartment is painted garish red and garish blue. It is insufferably dark, except for the front room on the street. We have to cover the window. It is insufferably hot with virtually no ventilation. It is a palace for us, a wealth of space. Off the kitchen is a thin wooden door, no lock, just a wooden latch. Through it is a toilet, shared with the next door apartment, also a storefront but vacant.

Before Juan comes, we are in the kitchen talking about our movie. We are going to make a movie, a tough, unsentimental avant-garde little number about women in a New York City prison. I have written it. It strangely resembles my own story: jailed over Vietnam the woman is endlessly strip-searched and then mangled inside by jail doctors. N will make it—direct it, shoot it, edit it. It is her film. R is the star. She is N's lover for years, plans on forever, it is on the skids but she hangs on, pretending not to know. She is movingly loyal and underneath pathetically desperate. N and I are not allowed to be lovers so we never are, alone. We evade the spirit of the law. N refuses to make a political film. Politics, she argues, is boring and temporary. Vietnam will be over and forgotten. A work of art must outlast politics. She uses words sparingly. Her language is almost austere, never ornate. We are artists, she says. I am liberal with her. She always brings out my generosity. I take no hard line on politics. I too want art. We need money. Most of ours goes for cigarettes, after which there isn't any left. We fuck for drugs. Speed is cheaper than food. We fuck for pills. We fuck for prescriptions. We fuck for meals when we have to. We fuck for drinks in bars. We fuck for tabs of acid. We fuck for capsules of mescaline. We fuck for loose change. We fuck for fun. We fuck for adventure. We fuck when we are hot from the weather. We fuck for big bucks to produce our movie. In between, we discuss art and politics. We listen to music and read books. She plays sax and clarinet and I write short stories. We are poor but educated.

*

The day we moved in the men, our neighbors, paid us a visit. We will get you, they said. We will come when we are ready. We will fuck you when we are ready. We will come one night when we decide. Maybe we will sell you. N is worth a lot of money in Puerto Rico, they say. I am worth not so much but still a little something. They are relaxed, sober. Some have knives. They take their time. How will you keep us out, one man asks logically. What can you do to keep us out. One night we will come. There are six or seven of them

41

there. Two speak, alternating promises. One night we will come.

Our friend M shows up then, cool cool pacifist hippie type, white, long hair in a ponytail. Hey man, he says, hey man, hey man, let's talk peace not war, let's be friends man, let's have some smoke. He invites them into our storefront. The men sit in a circle in the front room, the front door wide open. Hey, man, come on, these chicks are cool. Hey, man, come on, these chicks are cool. Hey, man, come on, I got some good smoke, let's just cool this out man smoke some smoke man together man these are cool chicks man. He passes a pipe, passes joints: it is a solemn ceremony. We gonna come in and get these chicks when we want them man. Hey man, come on, man, these chicks are real cool, man, you don't wanna mess with these chicks man they are cool man. The pipe goes round and round. The neighbors become quiet. The threats cease. M gloats with his hip, his cool, his ponytail accomplishment as peacemaker. Hey man any time you want some smoke you just come to me man just leave these chicks alone man smoke and peace man, you know, man.

They file out, quiet and stoned. M is elated. He has forged a treaty, man. M is piss-proud, man. We get stoned. Smoke, man. The front door stays wide open as we sit in the front room and smoke. Night comes, the dark. M points to the open door. Just stay cool with those guys, man. Those guys come back you just invite them in for a little smoke. It's cool, man.

*

I have a habit, not nice. I am two years into it this time. I have had it before. Black beauties. I take a lot of pills. The pills cost a lot of money. N takes them too. I don't know if it is addiction or pleasure for her or how long she has been taking them or if she can do without them. I never ask. These are privacies I respect. I have my own dignity too. I pretend it is cheaper than food.

One night N brings home a fuck, a Leo named Leo. He steals our speed and all our cash. The speed is gone. I go into emergency gear. I pretend it is a joke. How the fuck, I ask her repeatedly, can anyone be stupid enough to fuck someone who says he is a Leo named Leo? I ask this question, tell this joke, many times. I am scared. We find a trick. She fucks him because

42

she lost the pills. It is our code and her own personal sense of courtesy. We get the pills. A Leo named Leo, I say. How can anyone be so stupid? We pop the pills. A Leo named Leo. We sit in our middle room, she is drinking scotch and I am drinking vodka, we are momentarily flush: and the pills hit. A Leo named Leo. We laugh until we start to cry. We hold our guts and shake. A Leo named Leo. She grins from ear to ear. She has done something incredibly witty: fucked a Leo named Leo. We are incredibly delighted with her.

*

Walking down St Mark's Place I run into an old lover, Nikko. He is Greek. I love Greece. We say hello, how are you in Greek. It is hot. I take him back with me. N is not there. We have a fight. I am insulted because he wants to wear a condom. But women are dirty, he says as a point of fact. I am offended. I won't allow the condom. We fight. He hits me hard in the face several times. He hits me until I fall. He fucks me. He leaves. It is two weeks before I remember that this is what happened last time. Last winter. Women carry diseases, he said. No condoms, I said. He hit me several times, hard in the face, holding me up so he could keep hitting. He fucked me and left. I had another lover coming, a woman I had been waiting for weeks to see, married, hard to see. I picked myself up and forgot about him. She was shameless: she liked the bruises, the fresh semen. He didn't use the condom. Either time.

*

We proceed with our film project. We are intensely committed to it, for the sake of art. The politics of it is mine, a hidden smile behind my eyes. We call a famous avant-garde film critic. He says he will come to see us at midnight. At midnight he comes. We sit in the front room, huddled on the floor. He is delicate, soft-spoken, a saintly smile: he likes formal, empty filmic statements not burdened by content: our film is some baroque monster in his presence, overgrown with values and story and plot and drama. It will never have this appearance again. Despite his differences with us—aesthetic, formal, ethereal—he will publish an interview with us to help us raise money. We feel lifted up, overwhelmed with recognition: what he must see in us to do this for us, a pure fire. We wait for the other shoe to drop.

43

But he sits there, beatific. We can interview each other and send it to him along with photographs of us. He drinks our pathetic iced tea. He smiles. No shoe drops. He leaves.

The next days we spend in a frenzy of aesthetic busywork. We take pencils in hand and plot out long, interesting conversations about art. We try to document an interesting, convoluted discussion of film. We discuss Godard at some length and write down for posterity our important criticisms of him. We are brassy, hip, radical, cool. We haunt the photo machines at Woolworth's, taking artistic pictures of ourselves, four poses for four quarters. We use up all our change. We hustle more. Excuse me, sir, but someone just stole my money and I don't have a subway token to get home with. Excuse me, sir, I am very hungry and can't you spare a quarter so I can get some food. Excuse me, sir, I just lost my wallet and I don't have bus fare home.

Then we go back to the machine and pose and look intense and avant-garde. We mess up our hair and sulk, or we try grinning, we stare into the hidden camera, looking intense, looking deep, looking sulky and sultry and on drugs.

We write down some more thoughts on art. We pick the photos we want. We hustle for money for stamps. Excuse me, sir, my child is sick and I don't have any money to buy her medicine.

The critic prints our interview. He doesn't print our photographs. We are famous. Our thoughts on film and art are in the newspaper. We wait for people to send us money.

*

We run back and forth from our storefront to Woolworth's as we get the money to take more photos. We run back and forth as we add pages and pages to our interview with each other. I sit at the typewriter ponderously. This is an important project. We run back and forth each time we think of something new to add: a new pose to try, a new sentence to write down, a new topic to explore, a new intensely artistic sulk or pout. We make feverish notes in Woolworth's and run home to type them up. On one trip a policeman follows us. He walks half a block behind us, keeping us in sight. We go faster, go slower, he stays half a block behind us. Girls, he calls finally, girls. We wait.

He catches up. There is a silence. Did you know, girls, that about half an hour ago you crossed the street against a red light? We are properly stunned, truly stunned, silent and attentive. I have to write you girls a ticket but listen I don't want to be too hard on you, I don't want to give you a record or anything so why don't I write it just for one of you. The three of us decide he will give the ticket to N since the apartment is not in her name. He slowly, soberly, prints her name out in big block letters. Now listen girls you be careful next time I don't want to have to do this again you hear. We stand there, dazed and acquiescent. We walk on slowly, once we are sure he is really gone. We look over our shoulders. Is he still there or was he really there? N has a ticket for jaywalking in her hand. Between us right then we have a dozen tabs of acid and a bag of marijuana and some loose joints. We have no money for food so we have been living on speed and alcohol. We have the speed on us, in a prescription bottle but you would have to be a fool to believe it. We are hungry and as soon as we mail off our interview we know we are going to have to find a fuck. We are stoned beyond all imagining, and yet of course intensely serious about art. Still, in the scheme of things, jaywalking is not a good thing to do. We can see that now, once we think about it. We think about it now quite a lot, rolling along the city streets in the burning heat, our sides splitting with laughter. We are dazzled with the universe and its sense of humor. We are dazzled too by its generosity: we are left to pursue art: we are not carted off, dangerous criminals, drowning in drugs. We are artists, not riffraff. We are scared, the cop's breath still hot on our silly necks. Hungry, we find a fuck, a safe one, N's girlfriend, to whom we recount our uproarious adventure, stressing our triumphant escape. She feeds us, just barely pretending to be amused. I leave them alone. N pays for the meal.

*

Poor R's apartment is tiny and dark, on the first floor of a brown brick building in a Mafia neighborhood. Italian rings out around us: is it apocryphal or are stolen bicycles really returned? R says it is true. She says she is safe here. Every window is covered in layers of metal. It is dark, but it is the real Village, not the Lower East Side. It is West. It is not piss-covered. It is not blood-drenched.

Poor R is refined, ladylike, devoted. She cuts N's hair and sews clothes for her. She makes her meals and feeds her friends. She is repelled by the company N keeps but she is devoted anyway, the soul of quiet devotion no matter what the provocation. She wants to be a refuge, a retreat, a nest. She makes sachets of delicate smells. She lights delicate candles to go with dinner. She cooks delicate soufflés and serves many kinds of cheeses. She goes to auditions and gets jobs off-Broadway in little theaters. She is small and delicate and refined. She is quiet and kind. She is genuinely devoted. We come from the dense torment of our storefront, immersed in the drugs, smelling of the sex, numb from the violence, nevertheless exhilarated: and she feeds us and lets us sleep: because she is in love and devoted. She is talented, carefully dressed, not pretty, not handsome, but each feature is distinct so that the face adds up to an expressive one. She reads books and listens to music, all in moderation. She loves devotedly, without moderation. She hangs in for the long haul. She is promising to be there forever. She wants to be there when N, weary, wants peace. Given half a chance, she would be the one. But she has no chance. N is bored. We eat, I leave, N pays for the meal.

*

N is easy to love, devotedly. She is very beautiful, not like a girl. She is lean and tough. She fucks like a gang of boys. She is smart and quiet. She doesn't waste words. She grins from ear to ear. She is never afraid.

*

Women pursue her. She is aloof, amused. She fucks everyone eventually, with perfect simplicity and grace. She is a rough fuck. She grinds her hips in. She pushes her fingers in. She tears around inside. She is all muscle and jagged bones. She thrusts her hips so hard you can't remember who she is or how many of her there are. The first time she tore me apart. I bled and bled.

*

Women want her. So do men. She fucks everyone. It is always easier for her to than not to. She has perfect courtesy and rare grace. She is marvelously polite, never asking, never taking,

46

until licensed by an urgent request. Then she is a hooligan, all fuck and balls.

*

She is slightly more reserved with men. When a man fucks me, she says, I am with him, fucking me. The men ride her like maniacs. Her eyes roll back but stay open and she grins. She is always them fucking her, no matter how intensely they ride. Me I get fucked but she is different, always just slightly outside and on top: being him, fucking her. The men are ignorant and entranced.

*

She dresses like a glittering boy, a tough, gorgeous boy. She is Garbo in *Queen Christina* but run-down and dirty and druggy, leaner and tougher: more used: slightly smelling of decay and death, touched by the smell of the heat and the smell of the piss and the smell of the men: but untouched underneath by any human lust not her own.

*

She is ardent and intense, entirely charming, a grimy prince of the streets, tough and fast: destitute and aloof, drawn to the needle: edging toward the needle: but she fucks instead most of the time: she likes the needle though: you can see it in her eyes, all glazed over: she stops grinning and her lips get thick with sensuality and dirty with greed: she loses her courtesy: she is finally taken over: the needle is not her fucking her: it is something outside her fucking her: and she dissolves, finally. I could lose her to this. I never think about losing her or having her, except around the needle. It is the only thing I am afraid of. I would do anything for her. I want to shoot up with her: her do it to me, tie the rubber thing, heat the spoon, fill the needle, find the vein, shoot it up. She demurs politely. She keeps away from it: except sometimes: she does not draw me in. She does it away from me: with other lovers: now and then: glassy-eyed and elated: not aloof but ecstatic: sated: when no one could even see, from day to day, that she had been hungry.

Or I couldn't see.

Or she wasn't: the needle just gutted her with pleasure: so afterward, in retrospect, one inferred that there had been a lack, a need, before the needle: but in fact she had been complete before and now was simply drenched in something extra:

47

something exquisite, heavy and thick like some distilled perfume, sweet to the point of sickness, a nauseating sweetness: something transporting and divine: something that translated into eyelids weighed down and swollen, lips puffed up, the cracks in them spreading down, the body suddenly soft and pliant, ready to curl, to billow, to fold: a fragile body, delicate bones suddenly soft, eyes hiding behind lush eyelids: the hard tension of her hips dissolved, finally. The way other women look when they've been fucked hard and long, coming and coming, is how she looked: the way other women look fucked out, creamy and swollen, is how she looked. The needle gave her that, finally: dissolved.

*

The jazz club is on a rough street, darker even than ours. It is low down in a cellar. It is long and narrow. The walls are brick. The tables are small, brown covered with a thick shellac, heavy and hard, ugly. They are lined up against the brick walls one right next to the other. You have to buy two drinks. There is a stage at the end of the long, narrow room. Jazz blares, live, raw: not the cold jazz, but belted-out jazz, all instruments, all lips and spit. There is no chatter. There is no show. There is just the music. The musicians are screaming through metal. Or there is waiting—glasses, ice, cigarette smoke, subdued mumbling. The music is loud. No one talks when the musicians are on stage, even when they stop for a minute. Everyone waits for the next sound. The smoke is dense but the sounds of the horns punch through it and push it into the brick. We are listening to the legendary black musician who according to some stories turned Billie into a junkie. I am wondering if this is as awful as it seems on the surface and why it is whispered in a hushed awe. He is a sloppy musician by now, decades later. He is bent over, blowing. He is sweating like a pig. His instrument screams. There is not a hint of delicacy or remorse. The music rouses you, the volume raises hackles on your skin, the living, breathing sound makes your blood jump, but the mind is left bored and dazed. Other musicians on the stage try to engage that lost faculty: they solo with ideas or moods, some sadness, some comic riffs. But the legend blares on, interrupts, superimposes his unending screech. We can only afford two drinks but the legend makes us desperate for more:

to take the edge off the blowing, blowing, blowing, the shrill scream of the instrument, the tin loudness of his empty spasms. The set ends. We want to stay for more. It is live music, jazz, real jazz, we want as much as we can get of it. We cannot come here often. The two required drinks cost a lot. We are at a small wooden shellacked table against a brick wall. On one side is a bohemian couple, dating nonetheless. On the other side, the direction of the stage, is a man. He is huge. His shoulders are broad. He is dressed very straight, a suit, a tie, a clean shirt, polished shoes. He is alone. I hate his face on sight. It has no lines. It is completely cold and cruel. There is nothing wrong with it on the surface. His features are even handsome. His skin is a glistening black, rich, luminous. He is lean but nevertheless big, broad-shouldered, long, long legs. His legs can barely fit under the small table. He is solitary and self-contained. He has been watching N. He offers us drinks. She accepts. They talk quietly between sets. I can't hear them, don't want to. I can see something awful in him but she is fascinated. I can't name it. His expression never changes. It shows nothing. I am instinctively afraid of him and repelled. N listens to him intently. She looks almost female. Her body softens. Her eyes are cast down. The music starts. He leaves. The legend sweats and blares and spits and screams. He is even sloppier now, more arrogant too, but we are drunker so it evens out. We leave at dawn. We walk home in the hot haze. Junkies make jokes at us. Men pee. Someone flashes a knife from a stoop. We are tired. We sleep.

We wake up in early afternoon. The heat is stifling. Today we are going to take the special acid we have been saving, N and me and poor R. I am excited. N says first she has to meet the guy from last night. She promised him. She just wants forty-five minutes alone with him. He comes in the dead heat of the afternoon. In the glaring heat of the sun he is still cold, glistening, mean. He wears a suit. He wears a tie. He has on a clean shirt, buttoned up to the top. His shoes are polished. His face is set, he doesn't try to smile, he has no expression, he doesn't sweat. Standing up he is towering, dangerous, cold. N is happy to see him, reserved, courteous. I am bewildered and afraid. I just want to fuck him, she says quietly to me. We have dropped the acid. He is dangerous, I say. What are you going to do when you start tripping? He will be gone by then, she says. One fuck, then he will go. I wait outside like she tells me to. They go into our storefront. I expect to hear screams. I hear nothing. I strain to hear but I hear nothing. Forty-five minutes later they come out. Nothing has changed with him. Suit. Tie. Clean shirt, buttoned up. Polished shoes. No expression. Still not sweating. N is glassy-eyed, creamy, content. I got what I wanted, she said. Whad ya do in there, I ask, casual but really scared, worse now since I see no sign of human emotion or exertion in him. Just fucked, she says. He is not a man who fucks. I can see that. He may kill but he doesn't fuck. Either the needle or he tied her up. I am pretty sure. She is wearing a blouse with long sleeves, not her usual T-shirt. I don't see her naked for the next few days. Even as the street begins to slide and whirl, I know that there are bruises on her arm from one thing or another. I don't exactly know the word sadist but that is what I think he is anyway. I strain for the word without finding it but I know what I mean. I am scared. She is satisfied. I never see him again. I think he kills people. Most of the violent men we see are sloppy, one way or another. Their violence sort of oozes out. This man is a perfect diamond cutting through glass.

*

There are the layers, the dumb, slobbering junkies, oozing pus and grief, dealing a little, stealing, falling down on top of whatever doesn't move fast enough; there are bastards a little colder, still oozing, and the pimps, who drool. There is a ladder of street slobber, so that the violence gushes out like tears or drips like a leaky faucet, but it is a mistake, not cold, ruthless art: as much accident as intention, not coldly calculated and perfectly executed. Then there is this other level. No fear. No ooze. No slobber. No exhibitionism. No boast. Nothing except serious intention, perfectly conceived and coldly executed, an interior of ice and a perfect economy of motion.

*

What has he done to her? The acid begins to grip and she will not say anyway. Poor R had left when she heard N was inside with a man. N is politely, resolutely silent. She will not budge. We are worlds apart and the subject is closed. Then we are awash in acid and beyond all human argument. We begin to roam the magnificent city streets and to play like children in their decaying monumental splendor. We range over these grand cement plains like wild animals, we dance up mountains fleet of foot, we rush down rivers dancing on the silver light of the rapids: each sight and sign of squalor is dazzling and unique: there is no language for this and sadist is a word even when you can't quite find it: and each and every human form shimmers in light and motion: the cold, cold man is more than gone or forgotten: there is no place in the universe for him: he is behind us now and time is a river, rushing on. The cement is a luminous rainbow of garish silver and blinding white coming out of the gravel, rising up like a phoenix from it: gold mixes into the stone from the heat and the scarlet from the blood is brilliant and intensely beautiful.

*

The air is spectacular, daylight, light that dances, a million shining fragments of light like tiny speckled stones: you could reach out and touch them except instead you walk between them, skirting their shiny surfaces, never feeling their glossy round edges. You reach out your arm to touch a piece of light and your arm stretches into the distance, it has the curves of a gracious hill and subtle valley and your fingers slide gracefully past each other, one then another then another, and they are gracefully curved, like a valley between two hills, a slight curve, slack but aesthetic and delicate. And the tips of your fingers touch the light and dance, dance.

The red from the traffic light spreads out through the air, it is circle on circle of diffusing red light, it is like a red light in the sky and with the sun behind it, it becomes fierce and hot. The streets are endless arcades filled with gentle refuges. There are stores where they greet you warmly, hippie boys all hairy and with wet eyes, and give you tea and have you sit and offer you smoke: and you laugh and laugh: or are deadly solemn: and there is sitar music and you get lost on each note and drift until the hot tea is in your hand: and you come back, treated like a holy traveler, an honored guest, by the warm hairy strangers. You look at the colored beads and the huge drawings of tantric intertwinings on the walls: and you are home here on earth, taken care of, given refuge: until you move on, the acid pushing you, the pulse somewhere calling you.

Outside it is dark now, and you roam through the streets until dawn when you watch the light come up. There are people you touch, their faces, their tongues, you slip behind cars or into doorways or spread out on suddenly available floors, mattresses that seem to just be there waiting for the simple traveler with legs that spread all wet. You smoke and smiling people hand you pills and you swallow them because nothing can hurt you now: and you stop cars with your acid smile: and communicate with your acid brain: and you watch something you could never look at before, a huge roach, a dead rat, and you are awed by its monstrous beauty.

Your sweat simply melts you and you take off your clothes somewhere with someone and you come and come and come: and laugh: and fuck: and smoke: and drink: and run, run, run: and smile: and the music is everywhere, in the traffic, in the rumbling of the heavy trucks, in the sirens, in the screeching wheels of police cars, in nasty motorcycles and in the sucking sounds of the dirty men who whisper cunt when you walk by.

And you talk, intensely. The universe. Reality. Light. Truth. Time. Dawn comes and you are hungry. You are coming down. You smoke. You sit on a stoop, tired and content. A man walks by. You ask him for breakfast. He takes you to one of the all-night restaurants run for the likes of you on the Lower East Side. The rabble are eating, all tired, all fucked out, all drugged out. It is beautiful, serene. You get orange juice and blintzes and sour cream and eggs and toast and coffee. The man waits. Hey mister, you say laughing, wanna buy us breakfast? He nods. Now you sit and eat and he watches. Now you are full. Now he pays the bill. Now you say, hey, mister, wanna fuck? You are still zinging on the acid a little but mostly it is over: back to business: of course mister wants to fuck.

*

N and I sit on the stoop in front of poor R's apartment. The light is just beginning. The dark is lit up from inside. The acid is beginning to soften, to lose its grip. We are still wavy, still floating, still charged, still porous, bodies floating in light and air: but personality is beginning to creep back in: we know who we are and where we are: we know that dawn is on its way: we know that we are hungry and have to eat: we know the acid is going: we know the night is over and the trip is over and pedestrian day is nearly here: we sit watching the dark becoming lighter and lighter: we sit watching a dead rat at the curb: it is indisputably a rat, not God: poor R is sleeping inside, she won't let us in, she won't make us breakfast, we are ex-communicated, we are happy, we are turned loose to look for breakfast elsewhere: we sit there, buddies, and chat in the dark: we walk around: we touch fingers and briefly hold hands.

*

N and I sit on a stoop in St Mark's Place. Hey mister. We are hungry. The acid is wearing off. The smoke has given us ravenous appetites. We are tired. Hey mister. Some misters pass. This one mister takes us to breakfast. He is silent, watchful, not easy to disarm. Mister turns out to be not such an easy fuck. N fucks him and falls asleep. Mister doesn't sleep. Mister probably hasn't slept in months. Mister is nuts. I get Mister for hours. N sleeps like a log.

*

Mister is white, lean, wiry, crew-cut, muscled, tense, wired to go off. A coil ready to spring. Full of inexplicable rushes of violence. He fucks like he hates it. It never gets him anywhere. He concentrates, he fucks. You can't feel much except his concentration. He is doing some martial art of the thighs, over and over, trying to make it perfect, get it right: it doesn't touch him: then the violence pours through him, impersonal, and he is in a frenzy of fuck: then, more tense but calmer, he concentrates, he fucks. Eventually I sleep. I don't know how or why.

When I wake up it is nearly night again. He is taking us to the beach. The heat here in the storefront is scalding; treacherous, wet steam. Our skin is raw and burning. Our clothes are wet. Our eyes are almost swollen shut. It is hard to breathe. Heat hurts our lungs. Mister has a car. He is giving us dinner. We are going with him to the beach.

He drives like a maniac, but we only feel the breeze. The car barely touches the road. It swerves. We leave the city behind. The air gets less hot. We see the city lights trailing behind us as we swerve and curve in the airborne car. We cool down enough to be afraid.

The car stops, and there is a beach and an ocean. It is end-lessly deserted. There are no cars. There are no people. There is a full moon and it is nearly light on the beach. The water

53

shines. It advances up against the beach. The waves are small and delicate. The ocean is tame but it goes on forever. It goes out as far as we can see, way past the moon. We are on the beach. Mister wants some sex. N whispers to me that she can't fuck, she is bleeding again. All summer she has had this mysterious bleeding. I tease her that she wants to get out of fucking this creep. But still: she is bleeding, not menstruation, hemorrhaging: she can't be fucked. She and I make love for him on the beach. It is not enough. He is wired, tense, has spasms of violence, shows us his knife. N holds me down from behind, both arms. He turns away one minute, a modest gesture unzipping his fly. She grins ear to ear. I try to get loose watching her grin. She is strong and I can't. She holds me down. He pulls down his pants. He fucks me. I get dressed. N and I sit and watch the ocean. N and I sit and watch the moon. He goes off by himself. A cop comes along. What are you doing here? Watching the ocean officer. It's dangerous here at night girls. Thanks officer. We walk up to the car. The cop moves on. Mister jumps up from behind the car, plays with his knife. Mister takes us for lobster, he is silent and watchful, he doesn't eat, then Mister drives us home.

*

We get out of the car. The beach is there. The ocean is there. The moon is full. We see the ocean with the moon hanging over it. Mister is wired. Mister tells us he has a gun in the car under the front seat. Mister tells us he hates his wife. Mister tells us he is going to kill the bitch. Mister tells us his wife has tried to get away from him. Mister tells us his wife was walking down a street and he beat the bitch to pieces and pulled a knife on her. How could his wife do that, we say, not knowing what she did. We go on to the beach.

*

The beach is a little scummy, empty cans and empty bottles, paper, trash. The sand is a little dirty. N and I undress each other. We kiss. We make love standing up. He wants us in the sand. We make love in the sand. She dresses. He shows a knife. She holds me down. I am flat on my back naked on the beach. She is behind me. I look up into her face. She grins. It is her comradely grin. But I try to get loose and can't. She is strong. She is holding me down. It is our charade, but I can't get

54

loose. He fucks me. He disappears. I brush the sand off but I
am all gritty. I get dressed fast. N and I sit and watch the
ocean. N and I sit and watch the moon. The cop comes. He
tells us girls could get hurt alone on the beach at night. We are
panicked that Mister left without us. The car is still there. We
walk to it. We get in covered with sand. I can taste sand in my
mouth. Mister buys us lobster. He sits and watches, all tight
and coiled. He drops us at the storefront. Inside we drink iced
tea and sleep entirely embracing each other. We sleep and kiss
like it's one thing, wound round each other like the gnarled
branches of an ancient tree. She has stopped bleeding. The
sand rubs and rubs, hurting a little, we are drenched in sweat,
we sleep and fuck at the same time, not letting go.

*

Have you ever seen the moon, full, rising behind the head of a
man fucking you on a dirty beach? Have you ever heard the
ocean, lying flat on your back, your arms behind you, held
down, have you heard the sound of the ocean behind him, have
you looked up to see her broad grinning face? Have you ever
felt the sand, dirty and a little wet, all over, and kissed her
thighs and the sand? Have you ever kissed a bleeding woman
everywhere and tasted dirty sand and then watched moonlight
fall on a knife and been naked in the sand while he fucked
you, the full moon behind him, the sound of the ocean behind
him, and your wrists weighed down by lead, her knees on top
of your arms as she caressed your breasts while he fucked like
doing push-ups, but the full moon is very beautiful and the
sound of the ocean is very fine?

*

And then, alone, have you needed each other so bad that you
slept and fucked at the same time, the whole time you were
sleeping, what others call night, so close, so entangled, melted
together, wrapped around each other, sand biting your skin
rubbing in the sweat: and been at peace, happy, with time
stopped right there?

*

The narrow mattress on the painted floor is drenched through
with sweat, and the sand pricks like sharp, tiny bites, hurting,
and the room is dark and airless, and we are wound together,
sleeping as we fuck: a somnambulant intercourse: wet and hot,

barely on the verge of consciousness and not yet dream: the heat turning it into delirium: for all the hours of a human night.

*

We wash. N goes to use poor R's shower. She has broken the letter of the law but will not tell. The promise was made when N loved her. Now she doesn't. The shower is redundant in the wet heat but it will get rid of the sand. I stand in our kitchen, it is dark even though sunlight blankets the earth outside the iron bars covering the kitchen windows: I look first through the grating over the doors and windows into the backyard to see if the neighborhood boys are there: they stare in, bang on the windows, bang on the doors: we try not to undress in front of them. I fill a big pot full of water. It comes out of the tap sweaty. I dip an old washcloth in and out of the pot and rub it disconsolately all over. Then I do the same again, using soap, but not too much, because you can never quite get it off. Then I do it again with clean water. Then I am ready.

N comes back clean. She has not told, I can tell. We both broke our promise to poor R. The beach was within the law; the whole private night was not. I am pleased. It is never mentioned again. Today is uptown business. The days of uptown business are few and far between, but all the same somehow. We are going uptown to talk with men who have money about our film.

N dresses. She wears a silk scarf as a headband and flared sailor pants. Her eyes are elongated and blackened and her lips are pursed: they seem longer, thinner, as if she is sucking them in. I too go out of my way. Clean T-shirt. Her hair is dirty blonde and straight; it stands up on end. Mine is curly and black; it stands up on end. We both comb our hair with our fingers. We make it stand up more.

Uptown there is a lawyer who is going to turn us into a corporation. He is silver from top to bottom. The spittle pours from the edges of his mouth as he listens to the details of our film. Of course he will incorporate us for no fee: but, leaning over, and over, and over, almost stretching the trunk of his body further than it could possibly go, *but*, he will expect to come to the Village for a private screening. Village, private screening. Saliva pours out, a thin, dripping creek.

Uptown there is a producer: will he sign N up and make her a movie star and then we can make our film with that money? Someone who discovered a famous rock singer sends us to him. We wait in the chilly waiting room. The sweat and the dirt that never comes off is pasted on by the cool air of the air conditioner. The men in suits and the women with lacquered hair and neat blouses and modest skirts stare. The receptionist is visibly disturbed. Inside the office is huge. It seems the producer is a quarter mile away. His huge desk is at the end of the huge room. We are told to sit on a sofa near the door. He tells N she isn't feminine. I say unisex is in. I say times have changed. I say people are riveted by the way N looks. The producer keeps staring at her. He talks and stares. He is hostile. She mumbles like Marlon Brando. The door opens. His wife, a famous singer but not a star, comes in. She looks old. She is dyed blond. Her skirt is short, way above her aging knees. Her makeup is serious. Each detail is meant to remind one of youth. Each detail shows how old her face is and how tired her soul is. The old legs on top of the high heels bounce under the short skirt as she makes her way across the huge room to kiss the producer. This is a woman, he says. You see what I mean, he says, this is a woman. We stare.

Uptown there is an advertising executive: he wants to give money to bright young men who want to make films. We sit in his small office. It is chilly. He stares. We discuss the film scene by scene. He discusses his advertising campaigns scene by scene. He stares. We ask for money. We leave the script with him. We are hopeful. N isn't really. I am. She is right.

The air conditioning always helps.

The offices are strange places.

The people in them seem dead.

It is the straight world of regular USA.

We abhor it.

We go back to our world of slime and sex tired and bored: to be alive as we understand living. *Not like them.*

*

The world is divided that way now: the straight adults, old people; and us. It is that way.

*

On St Mark's Place the police are always out in large numbers, hassling the hippies. Where we live there are never any police, no matter who gets hurt or how bad. It takes a riot to bring them out. Then they shoot.

The flower girls and boys abound in other parts of the neighborhood, not near us.

We are not them and not not them. N grew up in a swamp in the South, oldest child, four boys under her, father abandoned family, became a religious fanatic after running whores for a while, came back, moved the family North, sent her to a girls' school to get a proper upbringing, then ran off again: like me, poor and half orphaned. Like me she gets a scholarship to a rich girls' college. We meet there, the outcast poor, exiled among the pathetic rich. We don't have money hidden away somewhere, if only we would behave. Her mother, my father, have nothing to give. She has other children to feed. He is sick, says nothing, does nothing, languishes, a sad old man with a son killed in Vietnam and a dirty daughter on dirty streets. N and I are poor now: poorer even than when we were children: nothing but what we get however we get it. But also we are white and smart and well-educated. Do we have to be here or not?

We can't be lacquer-haired secretaries. There is no place else for us. The flower children are like distant cousins, the affluent part of the family: you hear about them but it doesn't mean you can have what they have. They wear pretty colors and have good drugs, especially hallucinogens, and they decorate the streets with paint and scents: incense, glitter: fucking them is fun sometimes but often too solemn, they bore with their lovey pieties: but we didn't leave anything behind and we got nothing to go back to.

*

Eighteen, nineteen, twenty: those years. The men numbered in the thousands. At first I was alone, then, with her, I wasn't. This was one summer. We also had a winter and a spring before.

*

Every time we needed petty cash: and when we didn't.

*

We took women for money too, but with more drama, more plot, more plan. They had to be in love or infatuated. You had

58

to remember their names and details of their childhood. They gave you what you needed gingerly: the seduction had to continue past sex: sometimes they would get both of us: other times only one of us could get near enough: or sometimes we would both be there, each one picking up the slack when the other got bored, and take turns before drifting off to sleep. Or N would do it one night, me another. I liked another woman's body there between us, and I liked when N fucked me then her and then I kept kissing her between the legs, though N would have fallen asleep by then. I liked those nights. I didn't like that we never got enough out of it: enough money: enough food: enough: and I didn't like it that the women got clingy or all pathetic or that not one could bear to remember how she had come, wanting to be courted, and stayed.

*

And then there was just having the women: because you wanted them: because it was a piece of heaven right in the middle of hell: because they knew your name too: because you went mad with them in your mouth: and you went crazy thigh to thigh: and it was earth, sublime: and the skin, pearl: and the breasts: and coming, coming, coming.

*

Especially the hairs that stayed in your mouth, and the bites they left.

*

The men fucked or did whatever: but the women came close to dying, with this quiet surprise.

*

And you did too, because you were the same, only harder, not new. They were enough like you. As close as could be. Every slight tremble shot through both bodies. Even when she knew nothing and you knew everything: even when you did it all: your fingers on her, her taste all over you, pushed you so far over the edge you needed drugs to bring you back. The small of her back, trembling: how small they were, how delicate, the tiny bones, how they almost disappeared: and then the more ecstatic exertions of a lover with her beloved.

*

The sex could go on until exhaustion defeated the prosaic body: these were not the short, abrupt times of men with their push and shove: these were long, hot, humid times, whole seasons: but once over, life went on: she was on her own, desolate: unhappy: ready to shell out what you needed so as not to be alone forever: so as to be able to come back: and you must never take too much, she must not be humiliated too much: and you must make sure she knows that you know her name and her uniqueness: and you must stay aloof but not be cold: and she gives you something, money is best: and she is just unhappy enough when she leaves. Her body still trembles and she is as pale as death, washed out, delicate and desperate, she has never done anything like this before, not wanting her own life, wanting ours: which we hold for ransom. She can get near it again, if we let her: if she has something we need. We are tired of her and want her gone. We are both cold and detached and ready for someone new.

*

The coffeehouse has a jukebox N likes. The music blares. She knows how to turn them up. In any bar she can reach behind, wink at the bartender, and turn up the music. In this coffeehouse, all painted pink, there is no resistance. It is in the Village, a dumpy one surrounded by plusher places for tourists and rich hippies and old-time bohemians who have learned how to make a living from art.

There is nightlife here, and money, and N and I hang out for the air conditioning and to pick up men. It is easy pickings. She roams around the room, a girl James Dean, toward the jukebox, away from the jukebox, toward it, away from it, her cigarette hanging out of her slightly dirty mouth, her hips tough and lean, her legs bent at the knees, a little bowlegged, opened up. She is dirty and her eyes have deep circles set in fragile, high cheekbones. She spreads her arms out over the breadth of the jukebox and spreads her legs with her knees slightly bent outward and she moves back and forth, a slow, ex-cruciating fuck. Jim Morrison and the Doors. Otis Redding. Janis. Hey mister, she says in her deepest mumble, you gotta cigarette. She gets courtly: I seem to be out, she says to him, eyelids drooping. She smiles: I guess I must of left them some-where. She hustles change for the jukebox. She hustles change for coffee. These are long, leisurely, air-conditioned nights. She disappears. I disappear. She returns, orders cappuccino, it means money, something easy with a boy. I return: we have sandwiches. She returns: with some grass. I return: we have dessert, chocolate cake, leisurely, cheesecake, passing it around. She returns: drinks for tomorrow night. I return: speed for tomorrow. We are bankers, saving up, past our immediate needs. She returns: some money toward the rent. She walks around the room, her hips very, very tough. The cigarette dangles. The music plays. Friends drop in and visit. She gets a glint in her eye: disappears: comes back to buy a round of coffees, some cake, some sandwiches.

Outside it is crowded, dark, hot, the sticky wet of the city air. The streets are overrun with tourists. The tourist joints are flowing over. They come to see this life.

Too hot to hang out on a stoop: so we go to the West Village to a bright pink coffeehouse, especially on weekends, rich tourists, rich hippie types, and then, at the end, when only the scum is left hovering in doorways, just plain punks who wanna fuck.

N returns: she orders a milkshake, sodas, buys cigarettes.

Poor R is going to join us for a cup of coffee: and someone N has met on the street, A. He is not tall, not short, thin but not noticeably, nice face but nothing special, intense big brown eyes, Brazilian. He is street stuff, not the idle rich, but with manners. There is polite conversation all around. Poor R considers this a formal date with N. A is there to meet me, to win my approval, because he is N's new friend, picked up on the street but she likes him or I wouldn't be meeting him now. The walls are pink and dirty. The air conditioning is not doing so good. The place is crowded. There is only money for coffee: we have coffee: and coffee: and coffee. N and poor R disappear, round the corner a block away to R's apartment: a date. A and I talk. It is working out. He has a lot to say. I don't mind listening. It is a sad story. Something about how he was a dancer and in love with a beautiful virgin in Brazil but her parents oppose their marriage and so he goes on tour and is in an accident and loses his hand and has punctures all over his body. He only has one hand. Then about his months in the hospital and how he couldn't work anymore as a dancer and how the girl left him because he was maimed and how he was arrested for something he didn't do and ran away from the country altogether and became a fugitive because he couldn't make anyone believe him, it was a murder he was wanted for. He was an artful storyteller because this story took nearly four hours to tell. I cried. His accent was thick. He spoke softly and deliberately. He didn't live around here. He lived around Times Square. Yeah he had some women out working for him: old girlfriends but no one he was living with now: but with N it was different. She comes back without poor R but loaded with money: poor R got two-timed again: and we drink coffee and eat and have more coffee and we talk there in the pink coffeehouse, the jukebox gone quiet. Outside the streets are emptying, it is nearly dawn. I go to the storefront alone, thinking about pimps, nervous.

*

A sits in the coffeehouse wearing a coat, as if cold. He hides his arm. It is shrivelled at the elbow. He has tremendous politesse and dignity. He is not handsome and not not handsome. He has some gentleness. He smokes like N, like me, cigarettes one after another, but he holds them longer in his one hand. He does things slowly: sits very still: slightly stooped: black hair straight and framing his face in a kind of modified pageboy for boys. His lips are thick but not particularly sensual. He has watery eyes. His skin is an ochre color. He wears dark colors. He is intelligent, well-spoken: soft-spoken. When N and poor R leave he doesn't blink or flinch or react: he is harmonious with how we do things: he imposes nothing: he has a sense of courtesy not unlike N's: he seems removed from physical violence but he can't be. I watch every muscle move, trying to figure it out. He can't be. N comes back and orders food for us. Poor R manages a stunning ignorance: she has gone on a date with her lover, just like other girls on a Friday night. N had left her some hours before, I could see by the volume of food and the new packs of cigarettes and the new rounds of coffee. Actual loose dollars are taken out in a rumpled pile. N gives me some money and some grass and some cigarettes before she goes off with A. I walk home alone in the dawn, the streets nearly empty now, the heat beginning to build for the new day: thinking about pimps: a bit disturbed.

*

N and A are now officially friends and lovers. This means it isn't for money. This means he visits us both and talks. This means we listen to music together. This means he and N go off alone for whole nights.

He is concerned about us, down in this violent neighborhood. He is concerned about us, so poor, and for what? We should be making real money after all, not small change for drinks and pukey drugs. We should have enough to finish our film. He is quiet, gentle, concerned. He is worried for us. He doesn't think we are quite safe down here.

He seems to adore N. He is nice to me. He is a good friend. He brings presents now and then, something nice, a bottle of wine, like a person.

At night we roam together sometimes: meet his friends at some late-night joint: the jukebox plays Billie, and we sit while he talks to his friends, sometimes about us, we can't understand, especially to one of his friends, a Latino, dark-haired, big moustache, long hair, machismo. They buy us food. We meet here late at night. A is who we are with. No one asks us anything. Sometimes he tells us to play something on the jukebox. He gets us something to eat. It is friendly and not friendly. It is tense. What are we there for? The men look at us: make remarks we don't understand. They play music and smoke and stare at us. It is ominous. I don't want to be turned over to them. It seems possible. There is an edge somewhere. A sits there polite as ever, our friend. N seems to trust him. He sits and watches too. The blues vibrate from the machine. The room is tiny. There are two or three tables against a wall where we sit. A sits on the outside of the tables, we are blocked in against the wall, the men stand around. There are a lot of them, all crowded in, and then spilling over to the sidewalk. Billie keeps us company while the men stare and do business. We are quiet.

*

A's best friend doesn't say much. He never talks directly to either of us. N sleeps with both of them by now. She says they have quite a routine. She says the puncture marks on A's body are holes that go right through his skin. Sometimes she does their laundry or stays with them a few days.

*

63

N meets some of his women. She is not happy. They are real Times Square whores.

*

He seems to be keeping N separate, apart. He and his best friend share her.

*

One night he comes to the storefront all soft-spoken, a friend. He has been thinking about our situation. We are all standing in the dark dank middle room, near the single mattress. He wants to help us. He has an apartment in Times Square we can move into, both of us. We don't have to do anything for him, absolutely nothing. We can just come live there. N defers to me to say yes or no. I say no. I have been thinking a lot about pimps. He is unruffled. He is our friend. If we don't want to move in with him, it's OK. He will think of some other way to help us. He and N go off. I wonder if she is going to live with him. She does now and then, for a day or two. He is a friend. I know he adores her: I can see it. I can't see him pimping but for a fact he pimps for so so much for what I can see. I like him and she is loyal to him: her loyalty once given is not breachable: her code is close to absolute, unspoken, I have never seen it breached: it is his lost hand, the punctures in his body, his best friend and the routine, his courtesy and intelligence, and something in him irredeemably outside: she even does their laundry. I say to her, you know, N, about pimps. Don't worry, she says, yeah I know.

*

I would believe her except for the smack. She doesn't do it regular but who knows what it takes, not much. He is besotted with her but the smack is easy: and he isn't any fool. I ask N what his girls on the street are like. She frowns, looks down.

*

He shows me his drawings, pen sketches, elaborate and skillful, images of horror and death. I show him my poems: the same. N plays her clarinet. These are family times.

*

He sits in the coffeehouse, in the bar, wherever, as we come and go: bringing money back: he doesn't touch it and buys his own coffee.

*

What else can I do? he says solemnly. I can't dance anymore.

*

I wait for him to mention the apartment again: to seduce, to convince. Then I will know. He doesn't. He is either sincere or no fool. He is no fool but is he also sincere?
 Can a pimp be sincere?
 Ah, he says, not too often, I wanted to dance.

*

He brings N a silk scarf: and me a book.

*

I am wondering if I should sleep with him: but they are a real pair, boy and girl: she waits for him and he comes often. I take my cues from her. She is not obligated, as far as I can see: she wants him around: she really likes him, for himself as we say, a lot. He remains nice. I begin to think I am wrong about the apartment. Then I remember his girls. Then I think about N and smack. I keep my distance. She is loyal to me too. She won't go without me. I think.

*

He died, my daddy, kind man, in a poverty of loneliness and disregard. I was not a good daughter. Nothing came to me when he died. I took a bus to the funeral. The relatives who raised me on and off were there. I hadn't dressed right. I was dirty and hot. I only had pants. Him being dead wasn't the main thing for them: it was me, not dressed right. The cemetery was flat and ugly. There were weeds. I got back on the bus right away. I got back late at night. I walk into the storefront and I think fucking pig, what the hell is wrong with her, there are things thrown everywhere, papers all around all over the floor and clothes thrown all around and everything is a fucking mess. She is not there. I know she is out at a bar. I am pissed like hell. I keep looking around, unable to take the mess in. Then it registers. There is nothing left. Everything is gone. The records are gone, the record player, the sax, the clarinet, the typewriter, almost all our clothes, except that some are thrown all over, every fucking thing that can be picked up and carried is gone: I walk through the apartment: the metal has been lifted off the back door like King Kong had done it: it must have taken hours to do and had to have been done in daylight: the neighbors must have enjoyed it: and in the re-

65

frigerator there had been a bottle of vodka, that's all, and now
the empty bottle was there on the sink. The fucks had drunk
the fucking vodka. There is nothing left, and at the same time
an indescribable mess of strewn things, like junk, trash, like
garbage.

I go to the bars to find N. She is far east, at a rough place I
have gone to long before I even knew her—I am two years
older and show it—and the bars are littered with my lost late
adolescence—I find her—I have fucked all the bartenders in
this bar and the one she is talking to now is the best—and I
grab her and take her home. She is pissed with me until she
sees. It is impossible to calculate our loss. Everything we own.
They ravaged it. Went through. Decimated it. There hadn't
been much until it was gone. I barely saw the damage the
first time. Barely saw what was gone. Barely remembered what
had been there. We have nothing left, except some T-shirts.
They have even taken underwear and blue jeans. They have
taken belts. They have taken everything.

The next morning our neighbors all greet us with smiles.

The next morning the boys across the street ask us how things
are going.

The next morning the head of the pack smiles and says hi
girls, next time we gonna come for you.

*

We are sleeping on the narrow mattress in the day. Next door
there is a thunderous sound. The thunderous sound moves
from one end of the apartment to the other and back again.
There are screams and laughs and things crash and break. The
feet are loud and fast, running back and forth. There is only a
thin wooden door between us and the next apartment. The
sound is very loud. It is not precisely human, not identifiably
human: it could be anything: like what? a herd of buffalo: we
are drifting off back to sleep: we dismiss it: it can't be anything:
it is broad daylight: the sound is thunderous, back and forth,
back and forth: we sleep. Later, we go in. They have been
there, while we slept, in broad daylight. Everything is gone
except for what they left broken so we could see it good. They
didn't take the TV that was in there. Instead they smashed it.

Hey girls we coming for you.

A knock on our door: head of the pack: hey we gonna pay

you girls a visit soon. You ready for us. We gonna have a good time. He leans against the door. He smiles. I start to close the door. He stops me, still leaning. Hey girl that ain't gonna help. Ain't nothin gonna help. We coming right in. When we ready.

*

It is having been asleep, hearing them, hearing the smashing, hearing the plundering, hearing the raucous laughs: hearing: while out cold: in a coma of sleep: having seen their knives: knowing them: sleeping through it but hearing it all the same. They will come: when they ready.

*

I beg N not to go out but she has a date with R. I don't really beg, it isn't in our code, but I ask, unlikely enough. I ask once. To my way of thinking, it is begging, don't leave me here alone. She wants to go, to get out, to get away, with safe little R in her safe little apartment. She is afraid. Don't go.

*

I bolt the door behind them, thinking where I can go. The banging starts. Knocking first. Then banging. The front door. Hey you got no manners you don't open the door. Hey it go worse for you if you don't open the door. Hey you want we break it down. Hey you want we come in from next door. Hey you want we use the back door girl. Banging. Banging. Silence. Hey girl. Just wanna talk girl you ain't gonna do no better than that. You got thirty seconds girl then we come through the front window girl: it break like a bone girl: you ever see a bone break girl I gonna show you how you arm break girl: and I got my boys in the back too you know that girl. I go to the phone: police, even though they won't come: the line is cut: the phone is dead. The back is a jungle.

I open the door. The head of the pack is there. Behind him there are seven or eight men, slouching, spitting, smoking. They are several feet behind him. He is smaller than most of them, dark, curly hair, not shaved, heavy moustache, earring in one ear, gold, big dark eyes. Now girl this is the way it is, I keep my word, you open the door we talk. Now you make a choice girl. See these boys do what I say and now you let me in and you take care of me real nice girl right now and we have a good time or you close the door girl and we come in all together and we get you good girl: you see girl you decide. He pulls out a knife: gold, ornate, the size of a dagger. He fingers it. What do you want, I say. He says, hey girl I just wanna come in, have a little smoke, make a little love girl what you think, but these boys here they ain't so nice as me they a little rough girl sometimes they ain't so nice but you take my word girl you let me in and I tell them to go home and they go home. I don't know what he will do but I know what they will do. I take my chances with him. I say, you have to leave the knife outside. He says, no girl hey that knife she my friend she go with me where I go girl. I say, I won't let you in with the knife. OK, girl, I put the knife right here, right on this here window girl, and if anything happen to me girl my boys put this knife right in your back you understand girl. I nod. He turns to them, says something in Spanish. They linger. He talks again. They leave. Ah you see girl you so sweet it hard for them to go but you a friend of Joe now.

He saunters in, looks around. Oh yeah girl they was nice records you had, nice. He saunters into the middle room, sits on the mattress, takes off his shirt. A gold cross glimmers in his hairy chest. Hey girl now you make me something to eat, I got to have something to eat girl so I can screw you good. We got time girl. We got all night. We don't have much food, I say. Oh yeah girl that right, well, what you got. I say, there are hot dogs. You make me hot dogs girl. I want you to make me hot dogs girl. I am counting the minutes, thinking that maybe if I can keep him eating or talking or distracted N will come back or it will get light or he will fall asleep or I will think of something: I use pacifist strategies, try to make him see I am human, ask him questions about himself. The boys still outside girl, I holler and they come, so you cook girl. I cook.

He chatters. He grabs a sharp knife in the kitchen: hey girl this for me not you. You thinking about using this on your boyfriend Joe, that ain't right girl. He eats. Why you not eating girl? I say I am not hungry. I sit across the huge wooden table from him, the kitchen dull in the artificial light of a bare bulb. He eats. Oh this is good girl, you this good girl? We gonna find out girl.

He drinks iced water. He drinks iced tea. He drinks vodka out of the bottle. He gets up. OK girl you come.

He saunters back to the mattress. He takes off his pants. I

stand there. There is a banging on the door. I am frozen. Don't
you say nothing girl or you gonna be dead. The sharp knife is
in his hand. I stand there, quiet, so still. The knocking continues. You know who that is girl? I nod yes, thinking that if I
can get to the door maybe I can get help: but afraid it is his
boys. The knocking goes on and on. I don't dare move. We
wait for it to stop. I say maybe I should see who it is. He says
don't you move girl, don't you fucking move. The knocking
stops. He says, now you get over here girl. The knocking starts
again. A deep male voice calls me by name. Oh, I say, it is
someone I know, if I don't answer he will be worried and do
something, but I can go to the door and tell him to go away.
You do that, says Joe real quiet. You better get him away girl.
You better do that. Or I gonna get you good girl. You ain't
keeping my boys and me out girl. I promise, I say, I will make
him go away. I promise I won't say anything. The knocking
continues. I see the knife, I see the cross, I see the hairs on his
naked chest. OK girl you got two minutes then you be here. I
walk toward the door. It is a long, slow walk and I am afraid.

I open the door. It is W, someone N and I know only slightly, a
dealer, a tall, thin, dignified black man: very tall. I step just
slightly outside the door and whisper please help me: I point to
the dagger on the window ledge: I say there's a man in there I
can't get out he forced his way in please help me I beg you. I will
take care of it, he says with enormous quiet conviction. He walks
in. Joe is there undressed, on the mattress, the knife in his hand
on his belly. W says, what's this I hear you fucking junkie you
trying to take my woman from me, I'm gonna fucking kill you.
He says this very quietly but with a deep resonance in his voice.
Joe begins to shake. Hey man I didn't know she was your girl
man hey I didn't mean you no shit man. He fumbles with his pants.
He fumbles with his shirt. He starts sweating bad. Hey man if I
know she was your girl man hey I wouldn't touch man it was just
a joke man. W says, don't I know you from somewhere man? Joe
says, yeah man, I buy some smack from you but times is hard
man. W says well you come to see me man if you need anything
but I don't want my woman here bothered. You understand, W
says with quiet seriousness and authority, this is my woman. You
treat her with respect man you understand she belongs to me.
Hey man I didn't mean nothing by it man.

Joe fumbles and sweats. They talk smack. Joe is sloppy and scared, W is austere and serious. W shows Joe to the door.

Then he comes back.

I thank him. It isn't enough. He tears into me. He bites my clitoris and bites it and bites it until I wish I was dead. He fucks. He bites my clitoris more, over and over, for hours, I want to die. The pain is shooting through my brain. I am chewed and bitten and maimed. I am bleeding. He leaves. I hurt so bad I can't even crawl. He leaves the front door wide open.

*

From now on N and I never sleep at the same time: one of us is always awake with a knife in her hand. We lie down on the narrow mattress together, never alone, and one sleeps and one stays awake, knife in hand, knife clutched, ready to use. She sleeps a few hours, I listen to every sound: knife in my hand. The sweat is cold now always: no matter how the summer heat boils and steams and hangs like fire in the air. I sleep a few hours, wake up in a cold sweat, always to find her wide awake, eyes wide open, alert, watching the room: anything moves, it dies. I count on her. I count on the knife. I think I can use it on myself, if there are too many of them.

*

We know they will come back. I knew Joe would turn me over to the others when he was done that night or some other. We know we can't keep them out. They know. We wait. We don't sleep very much at all.

*

I am staggeringly hurt: body and mind.

*

N and I are inside, sitting on the mattress. She is writing in her notebook. I am staring at the wall. I can walk now. There is a knock on the door. It is W. He is invited in. I don't talk. I sit. N sits. He stands, very tall, then sits. He brings out some grass. He is soft-spoken and courteous. He rolls a joint. We smoke. He and N exchange pleasantries. We smoke. I don't talk. He speaks directly to me. I stare. I haven't been talking much but now I don't talk at all. He saved me. I can't think of anything to say. I think I say thank you. We smoke. My body is slowly getting numb, hard to move, nearly immobile. Each arm, each leg, is very heavy, like a ton of wet sand. I can't move. I don't talk. We smoke. They talk. They talk about witchcraft, the occult, drugs. I don't follow it. He talks to her. I hear it. He excludes me but refers to me. He talks only to her. You young women need my protection. I could come here once or twice a week, get you young women a real bed, you shouldn't be sleeping on this mattress on the floor, so you really both sleep here do you? and you and I could have some real fun with her, we can do things of real depth, different things, unusual things that call on deep energies, there are many things you and I could do with her. I don't look at him but I know I am her. I can't talk. I can't move. My brain is some dead slug. Everything is heavy, like a ton of wet sand. My muscles don't move. My legs don't work. I remember crawling after he chewed me up, and the pain. We could do many things with her, he says, and there are mysteries we could discover together, she is the perfect instrument for us to discover these mysteries, she is so pliant, there are so many subtleties. He talks about a big bed, and I think he wants to watch N hurt me: he is saying they will do it to me, he is saying he will give us regular money every week, he is talking about a big bed and tying me up, I can't feel anything but the pain between my legs hanging somewhere in the center of my dead brain: telling me to run, run: but I can barely move: I concentrate every living ounce of will and energy on moving, one leg at a time, the other leg, slowly, to get up. It takes nearly forever. I stand up. My mouth moves. A sound comes out, loud. *No.* It sounds like a whisper. I walk, a ton of wet sand inching along a desert, into the kitchen, collapsing on the table. N says: you heard her. He says he will leave the grass and come back some other time. The offer still holds. N can call him anytime. But he will come back anyway. She should think about it.

All night we talk about a ring of occultists N has heard about and all the women they have tortured to death and their witchcraft rites and the way they use sex and drugs ending in death. She is sure this is true. We are afraid: we think it is a paranoid fantasy but we believe it anyway: we know somewhere there are these dead women. We do not move all night. The smoke has nearly paralyzed us. We fall asleep sitting up. In the morning N examines the grass to see why we couldn't move. She sniffs it and rubs it between her fingers, scrutinizes it. There are tiny fragments of glass in the weed: pieces of glass vials. The grass has been soaked in morphine.

I am scared. So is she, I think. I want to disappear. There is no money. I am too afraid for the streets. We are running out of speed. I cower on the mattress. She writes in her notebook.

*

I go to a junkie doctor in the Village for a prescription. I can't do the streets. He rubs his hands all over me. He is sweaty despite the air conditioning and old and pale yellow and fat. He rubs his hands up and down my arms and all over my breasts and my neck and up and down my legs, between my thighs. He rubs his hands all over my bare skin and all over my clothes. I sit still. He stares at me. He watches me as he rubs his hands all over. I am going to give you the prescription, he says, but the next time you come you understand what I want don't you? I stare at him. In the office there is a desk with a chair behind it and an examining table, the one I am sitting on. Here, I suppose, right where I am now. Do you understand what I want, he asks me again. I nod. I don't know exactly what he wants. I think in precise acts. I am going to write this prescription now, he says, and give it to you now, he says, but the next time you come, he says, you be sure you remember what I want from you. I nod. I am surprised, a little confused. I thought because he was a junkie he would want money. He doesn't ask for any money. I have in my pocket all the dollars we have. He gives me the script. He kisses my hand. I don't want to have to go back.

*

N has on her most flamboyant scarf, like a headband. She is carefully dressed: flare pants, a silk blouse A has bought for her, a belt fastidiously buckled. She has gone over the details of her appearance a hundred times. She is tired. Her face is drawn and dirty. Her eyes are lined with black, there are deep, dark circles under them. She is very thin. She is in constant movement, mostly examining herself, much motion to little purpose. She twitches with nerves on edge. A is in his usual dark coat. It is a hot night. I am going to stay with R, not to be alone and to be near a phone. A has thought of a way to help us. He and N are going to rob a store: a boutique to be

72

precise. N has some tools in a bag embossed with her last name. I tell her not to use the bag. I say perhaps they should not do this. It has been decided. N will call me when it is done. Our phone is still dead. No one stays there alone. I will be with poor R who does not know this is happening.

They go, I go. The hours pass. The night is long. A call comes about 4 am. N is on her way to the Women's House of Detention. She will be arraigned in night court.

Night court is interminably dreary and hopeless. The halls of justice are wide and dreary, the benches are wooden and hard: after an hour or so, a group of women is brought out: hookers and N, her scarf too high on her forehead, marking how many times she has rubbed her hand across her head, rubbed it back and forth, rubbing off sweat or as a nervous gesture. She is exhausted by now, but she can't sit still, even at the head of this awful room where she waits with the others. The others are mostly black with bouffant hairdos and vinyl miniskirts and bare shoulders and nearly bare chests. The others wear heavy, shiny makeup and high-heeled shoes. A Legal-Aid lawyer comes over to me, N has pointed me out: don't worry, he says, she will only do six months. I am like a demon possessed. She will not have to go to that prison, not this night, not ever, I will not have her there. Bail is set at $500 and there are two hours before she will arrive there, go through the maze of jails and holding cells and end up there, to be strip-searched and raped by hands, by speculums, by doctors, by police, by prisoners. I am in a frenzy. Bail bondsmen galore: I go to them one after another: I call up everyone for money: I get her out: I take her home. I go to an old friend who helped me when I was in jail: she calls a lawyer who used to be a prosecutor: he demands $2,000 but she won't do six months, she won't do shit. All this happens before I give a thought to A. He eventually gets two years. He protects her. He was a friend. Let's hear it for that sweet pimp. We have a lot of money to raise: have to get back to business. Can't afford to be squeamish.

*

The boutique, it turns out, belonged to a former lover of his, and *she is pissed*. She wants him prosecuted, won't budge. N could have gotten away, she chatted with the police for a while

73

before they realized anything was wrong: but didn't: wouldn't leave A there alone. He does two years, doesn't implicate her at all. We need money.

*

No more squeamishness about the streets. No more timidities.

*

Especially we try to borrow money, because we need it fast: from old school chums: it brings rich women back near us: near us: but we are too used, too disreputable now, for them to want to be that close: they help a little: they eat while we beg for coffee with hungry eyes: sometimes we get coffee. It is bitter: school chums: rich school chums: keep N out of jail.

*

A is gone from this time on. We don't raise bail for him. We don't go to court. We owe him. N is free. But we don't think about it now. We forget about him altogether.

*

We never sleep at the same time: one of us always has a knife. We eat speed. We pick up tricks as fast as we can find them. We drink as much as we can as often as we can: shot at a time now, can't buy our own bottles. The pace is fast. The fucks are fast. There is no time for style or pretense. We don't look around, ahead, behind.

We have been going four days straight: drink, speed, fuck, hustle, no sleep: the last night we took acid for R&R: we walked a hundred miles in the city and rolled in the sewers: the sun burns: we walk: we pick up what we can: bodies are giving out, tired: we are on our way home: we get home: she sprawls out on the mattress, I sit across the room: suddenly she says, I see something big and black crawling on you: I say, shit N it's the acid you just aren't down yet: she is quiet: she says, I fucking see them all over: and she is right: they are all over: huge water bugs the size of small fists: crawling everywhere: crawling all over us, all over the room, all over the walls. We run out into the night screaming, trying to rub them off us, feeling them all over us, inside our clothes, up our legs, in our hair: we keep shaking ourselves not knowing where they are on us, can't get clean, we are exhausted, we must sleep, no matter how much we tell each other they aren't on us we can't believe it, we keep inspecting each other but

74

can't stand still long enough to really look, we keep hopping down the streets kicking and scratching and twisting and turning, we feel them creeping and crawling, we bang on poor R's door, she lets us in, we vibrate from the acid for days.

*

An exterminator has put a pink powder all around the store-front. The water bugs now crawl around all pink. It is a spectacular effect. Eventually they die but nothing keeps them out. Especially they drown in coffee cups. The neighbors say they are coming back. Hey puta we coming. There is no money. The phone is dead. The walls crawl with pink water bugs. The heat hangs in the air like fire. In the bright glare of the day we pick up Jimmy. He is a masseur. He is thick and squat with muscles, black. He has no teeth. He comes to live with us, to protect us. N says I have to fuck him because I found him. I say I will because the neighbors are going to kill us: Jimmy brings his cat: sometimes she kills water bugs: other times they die in the coffee: I have to fuck Jimmy several times a day: it is not fun: N goes in and out: one night Jimmy disappears, N and I go out, we come back and everything has been smashed like maniacs have been through with axes: I say they are going to kill us, we have to get out of here: N says we have no money: I say we get it from one of our rich school chums, I say we call her and stick it to her: N is mortified by the implied or actual rudeness in this but I don't care: I call her: I make her come down to where we are: I say we are going to die here unless she puts us up in a hotel until the end of the summer: I make her take us to the hotel and pay for a room. We move in. I think we sleep for days.

*

The room has one window that opens on an air shaft. It is hot and stuffy. It has one closet. It has a sink. It has a very large double bed, for three at least. It is brown, with a lot of yellow in the brown. The bed has a bedspread, brown with a lot of yellow. There are two shabby chairs, a small desk, a telephone extension. Down the hall is the bathroom, the showers. The halls are grand: not plush but wide, marble floors, huge window at one end. We are off in a far distant end, narrow, as far away from the huge window as one could be. The woman next door asks us if we are on the circuit. I ask what circuit. The junkie

75

circuit, you know, she says, Tangier, Morocco, Marseilles, New York, Hong Kong. I say, no, we are not on that circuit. Our door stays open, for air.

The hotel is famous. Thomas Wolfe lived there. There are many kinds of rooms, suites for the rich and famous: rock groups stay there: and the maid tells us that down this very hall an old movie actor wrote his autobiography.

There is a rug on the floor too, brown with a lot of yellow in it.

Everything is dingy in our room: but the hall is grand. So is the elevator. So is the traffic: money and drugs.

N is bleeding again: it stops and it starts. We use our school chums more. They come here more. We are cleaner, calmer. We get dinners and various dates from them: they set things up: N needs a camera to shoot some footage, we are broke, the store requires a huge deposit, an old school chum finds a woman friend of hers for N to have dinner with. They pretend it is just regular life, like they lead: except they breathe faster.

There are things we have learned: principles we have discerned: now we let the men know we want each other, they can watch. We hold each other on the huge bed, we make love with each other: the men watch, the men pay: sometimes the men fuck but we can overwhelm them and they go soft, impotent: we have learned certain principles: we kiss each other, we tease, we hold out the possibility, we get dinner first, we get cash first, we get breakfast after: they are content to sit in the same room: sleep in the same bed: to be able to say they were there, it happened to them. N bleeds. We touch each other. A man watches. A man pays. It is easier on us. We use the women for money more and more: it is more artful: there is less sex.

When a man is not there, or another woman, we just sleep.

We make love, the man pays, the man watches, or there is just the hint that we will and he pays.

The footage gets shot.

We fuck less: N still bleeds: some nights we can't tell what the man will do: it is always a game of nerves: we play him: it is a game of skill: we do what's necessary: we start out playing our game not his: he still gets in, still gets the fuck if he wants it bad enough: N bleeds. Anyone we know we use for money. We find their weakness. We use them for what we need. We fuck their minds. We play with them any way we can: we take what we can get: but now we are selling something different, not the fuck but the idea of two women together, the promise, the suggestion. It turns out even more men are buyers.

We take acid, take mescaline, drink vodka. The camera breaks. We sit in a bar, 10 am, and start drinking with the $200 we have managed to collect. By 4 pm there is almost no money left. We are writing a letter to the Beatles to ask for money. We are drinking vodka martinis. We spill them all over the letter we have just finished and watch the liquid wash away the ink.

We go to an artists' colony. I am going to read poems. N is going to talk about the film. We want them to give us money. It is in upstate New York, rural, trees, air, the moon. We get there but instead of reading and talking we drop acid. We spend the next two days driving all over with two school chums, one of whom is not tripping, one of whom is having a bad trip, climbs under the van we have, won't come out, we drive to hayfields to sleep, we drive to the ocean, we undress, we swim, N raises herself out of the roof that opens in the van bare-breasted on a turnpike, we go a hundred miles an hour: she and I are happy: our school chums feel bad: we laugh: we watch every particle of light: we are happy: they don't forgive us.

We get the men: we make love: they watch: they pay. Or we promise, we touch, we flirt, they pay.

The hotel tries twice to throw us out for prostitution. I am indignant beyond belief. I scream at them about the First Amendment and the Bill of Rights. They desist, confused. What do whores know about the Bill of Rights?

We hustle day and night: we are busy: we have hit our stride: we get money: we hold each other tight and we kiss and we fuck and the man watches and sometimes he fucks one or the other of us if there is no way around it and the man pays. We anticipate them. We know them better than they know themselves. N bleeds.

She goes to the hospital. Her cervix is cauterized.

The time is running out in the hotel. Our school chum won't pay for it anymore. There is not enough guilt in the world to make her pay. N bleeds. She has acute pain in her side. She needs quiet, a place to rest. We need a place to live. We go to Staten Island to look for a house. The film is not yet finished. We find a house. It is raining. There are hundreds of steps up to it. It is up a steep hill. N is hurting very bad in her side. We want to move there, we have the money in hand, but how will we get more for next month and the month after? She is very sick. We have to leave the hotel. I take her to the Lower East Side apartment of a woman who has always wanted her. I deliver her. The building is a piss-hole, a stagnant sewer. The apartment is five flights up. In the hall there are caverns in the wall, the plaster broken away, with screen and wire covering them. Behind the screen and wire, as if they are built into the wall and caged there on display, are live rats, big ones, almost hissing, fierce. N is in acute pain. N bleeds. I take the money I need. I leave her there. I arrange to have pills waiting for me in Europe. The film isn't finished. N can't stand up. I leave her there on a soiled mattress, curled up in pain. I make her promise to finish the film. I don't think about her again. I don't feel anything. I take the money and leave on a boat for Europe. The great thing is to be *saturated* with something— that is, in one way or another, with life; or is it?

I love life so fiercely, so desperately, that
nothing good can come of it: I mean the
physical facts of life, the sun, the grass,
youth. It's a much more terrible vice than
cocaine, it costs me nothing, and there is an
endless abundance of it, with no limits: and
I devour, devour. How it will end, I don't know.

Pasolini

*

I can't remember much of what anything was like, only how
it started. No light, no weather. From now on everything is
in a room somewhere in Europe, a room. A series of rooms,
a series of cities: cold, ancient cities: Northern European
cities: gray, with old light: somber but the gray dances: old
beauty, muted grandeur, monumental grace. Rembrandt,
Breugel. Mid-European and Northern winters, light. Old
cruelties, not nouveau.

He was impotent and wanted to die.

On the surface he was a clown. He had the face of a great
comic actor. It moved in parts, in sections, the scalp in one
direction, the nose forward, the chin somewhere else, the
features bigger than life. A unique face, completely distinct, in
no way handsome, outside that realm of discourse altogether.
Someday he would be beautiful or ugly, depending on his life.
Now he was alternately filled with light or sadness, with great
jokes and huge gestures or his body seemingly shrivelled down
to a heap of bones by inexplicable grief, the skin around the
bones sagging loose or gone. He was a wild man: long, stringy
blond hair; afghan coat making him into some wild mountain
creature; prominent, pointed, narrow, but graceful nose; a
laugh that went the distance from deep chuckle to shrill hys-
teria, and back each calibrated niche of possibility, and walls
shivered.

It was amidst hashish and rock 'n' roll.

The youth gathered in huge buildings set aside for dissipa-
tion. Inside we were indulged. The huge rooms were painted
garish colors. There were garish murals. Political and cultural

radicals were kept inside, tamed, self-important, it was the revolution: big black balls of hashish and rock 'n' roll.

Inside there was this figure of a man, all brassy on the outside, and inside impotent and ready to die.

I took his life in my hands to save him. I took his face in my hands, I kissed him. I took his body to save him from despair. A suffering man: a compassionate woman: the impersonal love of one human for another, sex the vehicle of redemption: you hear about it all the time. Isn't that what we are supposed to do?

*

It doesn't matter where it was, but it was there, in a huge mass of rooms painted in glaring colors: rock music blaring, often live, old-time porno films—Santa coming down a chimney— projected on the walls, boys throwing huge balls of hashish across the room, playing catch. Cigarettes were rolled from loose tobacco in papers: so was grass: so was a potent mixture of hashish and tobacco, what I liked. I got good at it. You put together three cigarette papers with spit and rolled a little filter from a match cover, just a piece of it, and put down a layer of loose tobacco, and then you heated the hash over a lit match until it got all soft and crumbly, and then you crumbled it between your fingers until there was a nice, thick layer of it over the tobacco, and you sort of mixed them together gently with your fingers, and then you rolled it up, so that it was narrow on the end with the filter and wider at the bottom, and with a match, usually burnt, you packed the mixture in the papers at the bottom, and brought the papers together and closed it up. Then you lit it and smoked. It went round and round.

The boys had long, long hair. There were only a few junkies, a little hard dope, not a lot of stealing, very congenial: music: paint: philosophy. There were philosophers everywhere and artistes. One was going to destroy the museum system by putting his paintings out on the sidewalk free for people to see. I met him my first afternoon in the strange new place. He was cheerful about destroying the museum system. They were all cheerful, these energetic talkers of revolution. One spent hours discussing the history of failed youth movements in Europe: he had been in them all, never aged, a foot soldier from city to city in the inevitability of history. Another had Mao's red book and did exegesis on the text while joints were handed to him by enthralled cadres. Another knew about the role of the tobacco industry in upholding Western imperialism: he denounced the smokers as political hypocrites and bourgeois fools. Meanwhile, the music was loud, the porno movies played on the walls as Santa fucked a blond woman in black lace, the hash was smoked pound after pound.

The women stood out. Mostly there were men but the women did not fade into the background. There was M, who later became a famous dominatrix near Atlantic City. She was over six feet tall and she wore a short leather skirt, about crotch level. Her thighs were covered with thick scars. She had long, straight, blonde hair. She wanted to know if I had carried guns for the Black Panthers. Since I had been too young then, she wouldn't have anything to do with me. There was E, an emaciated, catty little thief: girlfriend of a major ideologist of the counterculture revolution, a small, wiry, cunning, nervous, bespectacled man: she wore government surplus, guerilla style: they were arrested for stealing money from parking meters. You can't make a great plan on an empty stomach, he told me. There was a bright, beautiful woman who looked like the Dutch Boy boy, only she lit up from inside and her smile was like sunlight. Her boyfriend was dour, officious, a functionary in the huge, government-run building that housed the radical youth and the hashish, he made sure the porno movies were on the right walls at the right times. There was Frau B, a dowager adminis-trator, suburban, having an affair with the head honcho, an ex-colonel in an occupying army: they kept the lid on for the government. And then I too became a fixture: the girlfriend, then the wife. The American. The only brunette. The innocent by virtue of Americanism. They kept Europe's feudal sex secrets hidden. I thought I invented everything. Smoking dope in their great painted rooms they seemed innocent: I thought I was the old one.

In these rooms, he looked up, his face all questioning and tender and sad: and I kissed him.

*

Once you want to be together in Northern Europe it is the same all over. There is nowhere to go.

In the South there are beaches and old ruins. Boys sneak girls somewhere, some flat place, and other boys hide behind rocks or pieces of ancient walls and watch. In the North it is cold. There are the streets, too civilized for sex. There are no rooms, no apartments, even adult men live with their parents. One is sneaked into a tiny bedroom in the parents' house: hands are held over one's mouth: no noise can be made: and sneaked out before dawn, giggling silently and left in the cold, unless one's lover is sentimental: then he covers you in his coat and buries you in his arms and you wait for dawn together. In Northern European cities, dawn comes late but parents wake up early. The young men have no privacy: they stay strange little bad boys who get taller and older. They get married too young. They sneak forever.

But it doesn't matter: where or why or how.

There were plenty before him in gray Europe. It was his sadness: saturating his comic face, his comic stance, his great comic stories, his extravagant gestures. It made him different: sad: more like me, but so fragile compared to me, so unused. When he looked up, so innocent, I must have decided. I became his friend, thinking that he too must love life fiercely, desperately: my gift to him: it costs me nothing and there is an abundance of it, without limits: the physical facts of life. There is not a lot I can do. I can do this.

*

Darker, grayer: no buildings filled with hash: another European city: to get an apartment: we had spent nights together out on the street, in the rain, in the cold, he was my friend, I had nowhere to go and he had nowhere to take me so he stayed with me in the wet nights, bitter cold. So we went somewhere else, Northern, gray, he came a few days a week, every week, he taught me how to cook, he was my friend. There was a big bed, one room, a huge skylight in the middle of the room, one large table in a corner: I put the bed under the skylight, water condenses and drips on it, but there I teach him, slowly. I have understood. He has too much respect for women. I teach him disrespect, systematically. I teach him how to tie knots, how to use rope, scarves, how to bite breasts: I teach him not to be afraid: of causing pain. It goes slowly. I teach him step by step. I invent sex therapy in this one room somewhere in the middle of Europe. I am an American innocent, in my fashion. I forbid intercourse. I teach him how to play games. You be this and I will be that. Rape, virgin, Queen Victoria. The games go on and on. There are some we do over and over. I teach him to penetrate with his fingers, not to be afraid of causing pain. I fellate him. I teach him not to worry about erection. I tie him up. Dungeon, brothel, little girl, da-da. I ask him what he wants to do and we do it. I teach him not to be afraid of causing pain. Not to be afraid of hurting me. I am the one there: don't be afraid of hurting me, see, this is how. I teach him not to be afraid of piss and shit, human dirt. I teach him everything about his body, I penetrate him, I scratch, I bite, I tie him up, I hit him with my hand open, with my fist, with belts: he gets hard. He does each thing back to me. He is nearly hard. Water condenses on the skylight and falls. We move the bed. I am disappointed. I liked the extravagance. I do everything I can think of to help him: impotent and suicidal: I am saving his life. We are on an island, isolated in this European city. There is us. There is the bed. He is nearly hard. We move back to his city, where he is from, into a room that is ours. He needs some act, some gesture, some event to give him the final confidence: to get really hard. Reader, I married him.

*

I love life so fiercely, so desperately: there is an endless abundance of it, with no limits: it costs me nothing.

Reader, I married him.

*

I thought I could always leave if I didn't like it. I had the ultimate belief in my own ability to walk away. I thought it would show him I believed in him. It did. Reader, he got hard.

*

He became a husband, like anyone else, normal. He got hard, he fucked, it spilled over, it was frenzy, I ended up cowering, caged, catatonic. How it will end finally, I don't know. I wanted to help: but this was a hurricane of hate and rage let loose: I wanted to help: I saved him: not impotent, not suicidal, he beat me until I was a heap of collapsed bone, comatose, torn, bleeding, bruised so bad, so hard: how it will end, I don't know.

*

Oh, it was a small small room with no windows: he had it painted dark blue: he didn't let me sleep: he never let me sleep: he beat me and he fucked me: I fought back and I tried to run away. The rest is unspeakable. He got hard and fucked easy now. Reader, I had married him. He rolled on top and he fucked: it costs me nothing, and there is an endless abundance of it: I love life so fiercely, so desperately: how it will end, I don't know.

*

Reader, I saved him: my husband. He can fuck now. He can pulverize human bones.

*　　*

I got away. How it will end, I don't know.

I love life so fiercely, so desperately, that
nothing good can come of it: I mean the
physical facts of life, the sun, the grass,
youth. It's a much more terrible vice than
cocaine, it costs me nothing, and there is an
endless abundance of it, with no limits: and
I devour, devour. How it will end, I don't know.

Pasolini

*

Sad boy. Sex is so easy. I can open my legs and save you. It is
so little for me to do. I know so much.

Sad boy. Desperate child. Gentle soul. Too much respect.
Afraid to violate. But sex is violation. I read it in books. I
learned it somewhere. I show you how: and I devour, devour.
There is an endless abundance of it, with no limits. I am a
woman. This is what I was born to give. How it will end, I
don't know.

*

Then I can't understand anymore. This isn't what I meant. I
am so hurt, the cuts, the sores, the bleeding, let me sleep. You
are hard now, my husband: let me sleep: I beg: an hour, a
minute. I love life so fiercely, so desperately: I mean the physical facts of life: I want to make you happy: I don't want to die:
the fists pounding, wild, enraged: sex was always so easy: it
costs me nothing, and there is an endless abundance of it, with
no limits: and I didn't want you to suffer, to die. How it will
end now, I don't know.

*

The bed: I show you everything: every wild game: soon we
drop the scripts and just tie the knots: how to penetrate: how
to move, when, even why: every nerve: pretending to pretend
so it isn't real: pretending to pretend but since we do what we
pretend in what sense are we pretending? You pretend to tie
me up, but you tie me up. I am tired of it now. I do what you
need, tired of the repetition, you learn by rote, slowly, like in
the third grade, not tone deaf but no genius of your own: the
notes, one by one, so you can get hard. You get hard. Now

you're not pretending. I don't know how it will end. I am waiting for it to end. I know what I want: to get to the end: you will tell me when the game is finished: is it over? are you hard?

*

He is normal now, not impotent and suicidal, but in a rage: my normal, human husband who gets hard: he is in a rage, like a mad dog. This isn't what I meant. I love life so fiercely, so desperately: I thought only good could come of it: sex is so easy: there is an abundance of it, without limits: I teach him what I know: he needed a little more confidence, so reader, I married him. I didn't know. I didn't know. Believe me, not them: the normal, human husband with normal, human rage: little girl saints of sex with your philosophy, little darlings, when what's inside comes out, be somewhere hidden, chaste, out of reach: it spilled over: it was rage: it was hate: it was sex: he got hard: he beat me until I couldn't even crawl: it costs me nothing, and there is an endless abundance of it, with no limits: I try to get away: how it will end, I don't know. Until now I devoured, devoured, I loved life so fiercely: now I think nothing good can come of it: why didn't someone say—oh, girl, it isn't so easy as it seems, be gone when what's inside comes out: impotence and suicide aren't the worst things. His face isn't sad now: he is flowering outside, to others, they have never seen him fatter, cockier, no grief, no little boy: the human husband, all hard fuck and fists: and I cower: reader, I married him: I saved him: how it will end, I don't know.

*

You can see what he needed, you can see what I did. It's no secret now, not me alone. I got inside it when it was still a secret. It is everywhere now. Watch the men at the films. Sneak in. Watch them. See how they learn to tie the knots from the pictures in the magazines. Impotent and suicidal. I taught him not to be afraid to hurt: me. What's inside comes out. I love life so fiercely, so desperately, and I devour, devour, and how it will end, I don't know. Sex is so easy, and it costs me nothing, and there is an endless abundance of it, with no limits: and I devour, devour. I saved him. How it will end, I don't know. There will be a film called *Snuff*.

I love life so fiercely, so desperately, that
nothing good can come of it: I mean the
physical facts of life, the sun, the grass,
youth. It's a much more terrible vice than
cocaine, it costs me nothing, and there is an
endless abundance of it, with no limits: and
I devour, devour. How it will end, I don't know.

                                        Pasolini

                              *

Sad, gentle face, comic. Unconsummated. My virgin. My little
boy. My innocent. Suicidal and impotent. I want you to know
what I know, being ground under: hard thighs: hard sweat:
hard cock: kisses to the marrow of the bone. I love life so
fiercely, so desperately. It costs me nothing, and there is an
endless abundance of it, with no limits, and I devour, devour. I
teach you. You get hard. You pulverize human bones. Finally I
know how it will end. Oh, I run, I run, little boy.

Coitus as punishment for the happiness of
being together

Kafka

*

I lived another year in that Northern city of Old Europe. Terror
wipes you clean if you don't die. I took everyone I liked: with
good cheer, a simple equanimity. There were houseboats,
saunas, old cobbled streets, huge mattresses on floors with
incense burning: long-haired boys and short-haired girls: I
knew their names: something about them: there was nothing
rough: I felt something in the thighs: I always felt something
coming from me or I did nothing: it was different: I had many
of them, whoever I wanted. I read books and took drugs. I
was happy.

I started to write, sentences, paragraphs, nothing whole. But
I started to write.

Slowly I saw: coitus is the punishment for being a writer
afraid of the cold passion of the task. There is no being together, just the slow learning of solitude. It is the discipline,
the art. I began to learn it.

*

I lived in the present, slowly, except for tremors of terror,
physical memories of the beatings, the blood. I took drugs. I
took who I wanted, male or female. I was alert. I read books. I
listened to music. I was near the water. I had no money. I
watched everyone. I kept going. I would be alone and feel
happy. It frightened me. Coitus is the punishment for the happiness of being alone. One can't face being happy. It is too extreme.

*

I had to be with others, compulsion. I was afraid to be alone.
Coitus is the punishment for the fear of being alone. I took
who I liked, whatever moved me, I felt it in my gut. It was
fine. But only solitude matters. Coitus is the punishment for cow-
ardice: afraid of being alone, in a room, in a bed, on this earth:
coitus is the punishment for being a woman: afraid to be alone.

*

I couldn't be alone. I took whoever made me feel something, a funny longing in the gut or crotch. I liked it. I took hashish, acid. Not all the time, on special days, or on long afternoons. I took long saunas. I was happy. I read books. I started to write. I began to need solitude. It started like a funny longing in the gut or crotch. Coitus was the punishment for not being able to stand wanting solitude so much.

*

I gave up other lovers. I wanted solitude. It took a few years to get faithful. Coitus was the punishment for a breach of faith.

*

I came back to New York City, the Lower East Side. I lived alone, poor, writing. I was raped once. It punished me for the happiness of being myself.

*

I am alone, in solitude. I can almost run my fingers through it. It takes on the rhythmic brilliance of any passion. It is like holy music, a Te Deum. Coitus is the punishment for not daring to be happy.

*

I learn the texture of minutes, how hours weave themselves through the tangled mind: I am silent. Coitus is the punishment for running from time: hating quiet: fearing life.

*

I betray solitude. I get drunk, pick up a cab driver. Coitus is the punishment.

*

I write day in and day out, night after night, alone, in the quiet of this exquisite concentration, this exquisite aloneness, this extreme new disordering of the senses: solitude, my beloved. Coitus is the punishment for not daring to be extreme enough, for compromising, for conforming, for giving in. Coitus is the punishment for not daring to disorder the senses enough: by knowing them without mediation. Coitus is the punishment for not daring to be original, unique, discrete.

*

I am not distracted, I am alone, I love solitude, this is passion too. I am intensely happy. When I see people, I am no less alone: and I am not lonely. I concentrate when I write: pure concentration, like life at the moment of dying. I dream the

89

answers to my own questions when I sleep. I am not tranquil, it is not my nature, but I am intensely happy. Coitus is the punishment for adulterating solitude.

*

I forget the lovers of Europe. They don't matter. The terror still comes, it envelops me, solitude fights it tooth and nail, solitude wins. I forget what I have done on these streets here. It doesn't matter. I concentrate. I am alone. The solitude is disruption, extremity, extreme sensation in dense isolation. This is a private passion, not for exhibit. Coitus is the punishment for exhibiting oneself: for being afraid to be happy in private, alone. Coitus is the punishment for needing a human witness. I write. Solitude is my witness.

*

Coitus is the punishment for the happiness of being. Solitude is the end of punishment.
I write. I publish.

*

Coitus is punishment. I write down everything I know, over some years. I publish. I have become a feminist, not the fun kind. Coitus is punishment, I say. It is hard to publish. I am a feminist, not the fun kind. Life gets hard. Coitus is not the only punishment. I write. I love solitude: or slowly, I would die. I do not die.
Coitus is punishment. I am a feminist, not the fun kind.

90

Ne cherchez plus mon cœur; les bêtes
l'ont mangé.
(Don't look for my heart anymore; the beasts*
have eaten it.)

Baudelaire

*

He was a subtle piece of slime, big open pores, hair hanging over his thick lip onto his teeth, faintly green. He smiled. I sat. Oh yes, and I smiled. Tentatively. Quietly. Eyes slanted down, then up quickly, then away, then down, nothing elaborate. Just a series of sorrowful gestures that scream female.

Gray was in the air, a thick paste. It was a filter over everything or just under my eyelids. The small table was too dirty, rings of wet stuck to it, and the floor had wet mud on it that all the people had dragged in before they sat down to chatter. I picked this place because I had thought it was clean. I went there almost every day, escaping the cold of my desolate apartment. Now the tabletop was sordid and I could smell decay, a faint acrid cadaver smell.

The rain outside was subtle and strange, not pouring down in sheets but just hanging, solid, in thin static veils of wet suspended in the air, soaking through without the distracting noise of falling hard. The air seemed empty, and then another sliver of wet that went from the cement on the sidewalk right up into the sky would hit your whole body, at once, and one walked or died.

I had nothing to keep the rain off me, just regular cotton clothes, the gnarled old denim of my time and age, with holes, frayed not for effect but because they were old and tired, and what he saw when he saw me registered in those ugly eyes hanging over those open pores. Her, It, She, in color, 3-D, fearsome feminista, ballbuster, woman who talks mean, queer arrogant piece. But also: something from Fellini, precisely a mountain of thigh, precisely. I could see the mountain of thigh hanging in the dead center of his eyes, and the slight drip of saliva. Of course, he was very nice.

* the stupids

Coffee came, and cigarettes piled up, ashtray after ashtray, two waitresses with huge red lips and short skirts running back and forth emptying them, and the smell of the smoke got into my fingers and into my hair and on my clothes and the rain outside even began to carry it off when it was too much for the room we were in. The empty packs were crumpled, and I began pulling apart the filters, strand by strand, and rolling the matchbooks into tight little wads and then opening them up all softened and tearing them into little pieces, and then I began to tear the fetid butts into pieces by tearing off the paper and rolling the burnt tobacco between my palms which were tight and wretched with strain and perspiration and I was making little piles of torn papers and torn matchbooks and torn cigarette packs but not touching the cellophane (he was talking), and making the little piles as high as I could and watching them intently, staring, as if their construction were a matter of symmetry and perfection and indisputable necessity and it required concentration and this was my job. During this we talked, of course mostly he talked, because I was there to be talked to, and have certain things explained, and to be corrected, especially to be set right, because I had gone all wrong, gotten all Dostoyevsky-like in the land of such writing as "Ten New Ways to Put on Lipstick" and "The Truth About How to be Intimate with Strangers." Coitus was what?

In the rain we walked to another restaurant, to dinner. Oh, he had liked me. I had done all right.

*

When I walked into the coffeehouse, he knew me right away. The mountain of thigh, not any other kind of fame. The place was wet, smelly, crowded, and I had picked it, it resembled me, not modest, dank, a certain smell of decay. The other women huddled themselves in, bent shoulders, suddenly, treacherously lowered heads that threatened to fall off their necks, tight little legs wrapped together like Christmas packages, slumping down, twisting in, even the big ones didn't dare spread out but instead held their breath, pulled in their tummies, scrunched their mouths, used their shoulders to cover their chests, crossed their ankles, crossed their feet, crossed their legs, kept their hands lying quietly under the tabletops, didn't show teeth, moved noiselessly, melted in with the gray and the mud and the wet, except for some flaming lips: and no monumental laughs, no sonorous discourse, no loud epistemology, no boom boom boom: the truth. I wanted to whimper and contract, fold up, shrivel to some version of pleasing nothing, sound the call: it's all finished, she gives up, no one's here, out to lunch, empty, smelly, noiseless, folded up. But I would have had to prepare, study, start earlier in the day, come from a warmer apartment into a cleaner coffeehouse, be dry, not wear the ancient denim articles of an old faith, witnesses, remembrances, proofs, evidences of times without such silly rules. He stood, nodded, smiled, pointed to the seat, I sat, he gave me a cigarette, I smoked, I drank coffee, he talked, I listened, he talked, I built castles out of paper on tabletops, he talked, oh, I was so quiet, so soft, all brazen thigh to the naked eye, to his dead and ugly eye, but inside I wanted him to see inside I was all aquiver, all tremble and dainty, all worried and afraid, nervy and a pale invalid, all pathetic need contaminated by intellect that was like wild weeds, wild weeds massively killing the gentle little flower garden inside, those pruned and fragile little flowers. This I conveyed by being quiet and tender and oh so quiet, and I could see my insides all running with blood, all running with knife cuts and big fuck bruises, and he saw it too. So he took me to dinner in the rain.

*

The bathroom was in the back, painted a pink that looked brown and fungoid, and I got to it by heaving myself over the wet boots strewn like dead bodies in my way, sliding along the wet puddles, touching strange shoulders delicately like God just for a hint of balance. The smoke heralded me, shrouded me, trailed behind me: in front, around, behind, a column of fire hiding me. The walls in the little room were mud and the floor was mud and the seat of the toilet had some bright red dots and green splotches and the mirror had a face looking out, destitute. I was bleeding. The rain and bleeding. The muscles in my back caved in toward each other furiously and then shot out, repelled. A small island under my stomach beat, a drum, a pulse, spurting blood. Oh, mother. I took thick paper towels meant for drying big wet hands and covered the toilet seat and pushed my old denim down to the slobbering floor. I

93

waited for life to pass, for the man to go away, for the blood to stop, to grow old and die. Four beige-stained walls, enough naked flesh hitting the cold edge of the cold air to keep me awake and alive, and time passing. Then I went out because I had to, because I wasn't going to die there, past the kitchen, a hole in the wall, burning oil hurled in the air by a cook who bounced from pot to pot, singing, sautéing, stirring, draining, humming. I walked through all the same tables, this time my hands straight down by my side like other people, and I sat down again. The piles of matchbook paper covered the table-top, and he was slumped and disbelieving.

*

On the right when you enter the coffeehouse there are un-appealing tables near the trash, and behind them a counter with cakes under cheap plastic covers but the cakes are good, not cheap. All the light is on the other side, a solid wall of glass and light, and all the tables near the glass and light were always filled with people with notebooks writing notes to them-selves on serious subjects as serious people who are also young do. I always looked over their shoulders, glanced sideways, eavesdropped with my eyes, read whole sentences or para-graphs. Sometimes there were equations and triangles and words printed out with dull blue ballpoint pens, like in the fifth grade, block lettering. More often there were sentences, journals, stories, essays, lists of important things to remember and important books to find. Sometimes there were real books, and the person never looked up, not wanting to be thought frivolous. Of course he had gotten a table filled with light, something I rarely managed to do, next to the glass, and the glass was colder than I had ever seen it, moist and weeping, and the light had become saturated with dull water. Outside there was the funniest phone box, so small it wasn't even the size of a fire hydrant, and there was a plant shop with the ugliest plants, all the same color green with no letup, no flower, no variation. The street running alongside the wall of glass was stones, the old kind of street, suffering under the cars, humans push ourselves on it and it moves under us, trying to get away.

His ears meanwhile flared out. His tongue splattered water. His nose was caked. His shoulders dropped, trying to find

94

China. His shirt was open to the middle of his chest, showing off his black hairs, all amassed, curled, knotted. It is not normal for a man not to button his shirt. God was generous with signs.

His fingers intruded, reaching past everything, over the ashes and butts, over the hills and reservoirs and deserts of torn matchbook covers that I had erected as an impenetrable geography, and they were so finely tuned to distress that they went past all those piles, and they reached mine, small, stubby, hard to find. Oh, his teeth were terrible.

All round there were students, archangels of hope and time to come, with dreams I could hear in their chatter and see circling their heads. Faces unlined, tired only from not sleeping, those horrible reminders of hope and time. Hamburgers were abundant. Serious persons, alone, ate salad. We drank coffee, this man and me.

*

I was appropriately frail and monosyllabic. "No." Soft. No.

His was a discourse punctuated with *intense* silences, *great* and *meaningful* pauses, *sincere* and *whispered* italics. "*Look*— I need you—to *do* something on *jeans* commercials—*Brooke* Shields—*something* on the *First* Amendment—I want—*you*— *to* talk about *little*—girls—and *seeing*—*their* tooshies. I mean—listen—*what* you—have—*is*—*terrific*—I mean—*I* know—*I know*—*how* good *it*—*is*—and I *don't*—*want*—*you*— to change—*it*. But the *country needs*—to know—what *you*— think—about *Calvin* Klein—which *is*—to—*me*—*frankly*—and *I*—tell—*you*—this—*straight*—out—*worse* than cocaine—and *I* want—*you*—to *say*—that. I want—*your voice*—*right*— *up*—*there*—*right*—up—front."

No. My *Crime and Punishment.* My *Inferno.* My heart. Soft, frail, no arrogance. "No."

"Listen—*I*—*need*—*something*   hot—*something*—like— *Brooke*—Shields—*and*—something *hot for* the lawyers—an— essay on the—*First*—Amendment. *I* mean—*I* know—*your* book—*isn't*—*about*—the—*First*—Amendment—but I need— *you* to tear—those *bastard*—*lawyers*—*apart*—and *something* on—*advertising*. I mean—The New York—*Times*—*is*—*as* bad—as Hustler—*any day*—and *we all* know—that—and *I* need—*you*—to say—*so*. And *why*—aren't *you*—*advocating*—

95

censorship—*I* mean—the bastards—*deserve*—it—and—we—
could get—some press—*on that.*

"*I need*—something from *you*—I mean—I—*can't*—just—
say—to the fucking salespeople—*I don't* have *anything*—on—
jeans commercials—and—I—don't—*have*—anything—on—
Brooke—Shields—and *everyone thinks you—want—*
censorship—so why don't *you*—just *give*—us—*that*—and
then—we can *sell—the* fucking thing. *I* mean—listen—I think
you are—right—*all the way*—I do. I—want—you—to know—
I *hate*—pornography—*too—more*—than—you—even. *I* have
my *reasons.* I mean. I don't think you are—*completely*—right
in everything—you say—*but* listen—*just*—add—*a few—
things.* You can have—*the* rest—I mean—listen. I am—*with
you—one* hundred—percent—*because—I—see*—what all
this—*does—to—women*—but—the thing is—*teenagers*—and
all those—*tooshies*—on tellie—in the—*living room*—and *I*—
mean—that is what *people*—understand."

"No. Thank you for seeing me." Soft smile. "Listen, I appreci-
ate your time, but no." Homer would die. Dante would shit.
Dostoyevsky would puke; and right too. Quiet, frail, polite, not
daring to show the delusions of grandeur in the simple
"Thanks, no."

I stand up and reach out to shake his hand. I am ready
to go. This is in the first five minutes. Then he begins with
literature, my heart.

*

He does the canon, my heart. Dostoyevsky, Rimbaud, Homer,
Euripides, Kafka my love, Conrad, Eliot, Mann, Proust. His
courtesy is sublime. Dickinson, the Brontës, Woolf, Cather,
Wharton, O'Connor, McCullers, Welty. Oh, I love them but I
have ambition like a man. I am curt, quiet, tender, bleeding,
especially quiet, but lit up from inside. He seduces. Dante.
Bach, the greatest writer. Months later I will finally read
Faulkner and he will be the only one I can tell, trembling in
my pants.

The next three hours are him, seducing, talking this passion,
I am building my little castles in the sand. Tess. Flaubert.
Hedda. Marquez. Balzac. Chekhov.

He wants to publish my book. As Is. It is bold and has
no manners. I am in life now confused, overwhelmed. On the

page never: but here I am dizzy, why does he, why will he, can he, is it true? Hush hush little baby, hush hush my dear. As Is. I am profoundly loved. We go to dinner in the rain.

*

Byron, the Song of Songs, Dickens, Mozart, Jean Rhys, Tolstoy and the Troyat biography and the new biography of Hannah Arendt, Singer, Freud, Darwin, Milton. I am profoundly loved. I am trembling. Donne. Utterly female. Bought and saved.

*

I am afraid to eat, wet, in the restaurant, out of the rain, trembling and wet: too carnal, too vulgar, too much the mountain of thigh, I want the ether.

*

It is, of course, not entirely this way. Somehow, Conrad reminds him of a high school teacher who had a boat in his sophomore year of high school; and Dostoyevsky reminds him of someone he fucked three weeks ago in Denver—it was cold there; and Milton reminds him of how misunderstood he was when he was eighteen; and Zola's *J'Accuse* reminds him of how he stood up to his parents and finally told them whatever; and Mann reminds him of a lover who told him how hard it was being German and of course he remembers the room they were in and the sex acts that went before and after the desperately painful discussion of how hard it is; and Virginia Woolf reminds him of how depressed he is when he has to attend sales conferences; and Singer reminds him of how his Jewish mother reacted when he told her whatever; and Mozart reminds him of all the piano lessons he took and how brilliant he was before he decided to be brilliant now as an editor of literature and also how he was unappreciated especially when he taught English to a bunch of assholes in the sixties who had no critical standards; and Freud reminds him of what it was like to be such a sensitive child in school when all the boys were masturbating and telling whatever jokes; and Jean Rhys reminds him that he has been stalled on his own novel for quite a while because of the demands of his job, which can be quite pedestrian; and Djuna Barnes reminds him of a party he went to in the Village dressed not in a dress like the other whatevers but in a suit and didn't that show whomever; and Dickens reminds him of how much he abhors sentimentality

97

and the many occasions on which he has encountered it and since he is in his late thirties there have been many occasions and he remembers them all. And the Brontës remind him of his last trip to England, which Maggie is really fucking up, which, he tells me sternly, is going to hurt feminism.

And I wonder how I am going to survive being loved so profoundly, like this. My palms do not sweat; they weep.

*

We went from the coffeehouse to the restaurant in the rain, wet. I tried to slide along the broken New York sidewalks, drift gracefully over the cracks, dance over the lopsided cement, not hit the bilious pieces of steel that jut up from nowhere for no reason here and there, not fall over the terrible people walking with angry umbrellas into me. I tried to glide and talk, an endless stream of pleasant yesses with an occasional impassioned but do you really think. We stopped, we breathed in the rain, breathless, in a crack I saw a broken needle, syringe, I want it a lot these days, the relief from time and pain, I keep going, always, away from it, he followed and we walked far, across town, all the way from east to west, in the rain, wet, cold, and I tried not to be breathless, wet, and the hair on his lip glistened with lubrication and he strutted, his shoulders sometimes hanging down, sometimes jutted back. They hung down for the Japanese. They jutted back for Céline.

The cement disappeared behind us, a trail of rice at a wedding, and stretched out in front of us, the future, our life, our bed, our home, our earth, wet.

We went into the restaurant, wet.

*

A small cramped table, an omelette, a dozen cups of coffee, a million cigarettes, one brutal piss after waiting all night, no dessert, his credit card: dinner: I was tired enough to die. Hours more of the canon, my heart. Except that we had reached the end hours before, but still he went on.

We walked out, I wanted to go, off on my own, back to myself, alone, apart, noiseless, no drone of text and interpretation, no more writers to love together as only (by now it was established) we could: just the dread silence of me alone, with my own heart. On cement, in rain, wet.

I left him on a corner. Asked him which way he was going.

98

Would have gone the opposite. Extended my hand, kind but formal, serious and sober, ladylike and gentlemanly, quiet but taut, firm and final. He took it and he pulled me into his lips so hard that I would have had to make both of us fall to get away: and I didn't scream: and he said he loved me and would publish my book. Oh, I said, wet.

*

We left the restaurant and walked down a wide street full of shops, cards, clothes, coffeehouses, restaurants, some trees even, brick buildings, light from the moon on the rain. We talked nervous clips, half sentences, fatigue and coffee, wet. We crossed a small street. We stood in front of a blooming garden, all colored and leafy, where a prison used to be, I had been in it, a tall brick building, twelve floors of women, locked up, a building where they took you and spread your legs and tried to hurt you by tearing you apart inside. A building where they put you in cells and locked that door and then locked a thicker door and then locked a thicker door, and you could look out the window and see us standing on that corner below, looking like a man and a woman kissing under the moon in the rain, wet. You could see the lights and the hookers on the street corners and the literati fucking around too. You could see a Howard Johnson's when it was still there and gaggles of pimps right across a huge intersection and you could hear a buzz, a hum, that sounded like music from up there, up on one of those floors inside that brick. You could see the people underneath, down below, and you could wonder who they were, especially the boys and the girls kissing, you could see everything and everyone but you couldn't get at them, even if you screamed, and inside they spread you on a table and they tore you up and they left you bleeding. And they tore me up. And now it was a garden, very pretty really, and my honey the publisher who I had just met was right there, in the moonlight, wet: and the blood was flowing: he grabbed me and pulled me and kissed me hard and held me so I couldn't move and it was all fast and hard and he said he loved me.

*

I am bleeding again on this corner; where there was a prison; where a man has kissed me against my will; and will publish my book, oh my love; and it is wet; and the cement glistens;

99

and the moon lights up the rain; and I am wet. I turn away and go home.

*

The windows were open, as always. The cold no longer streamed in as it had the first few months when the windows first had to stay open day and night: winter, fall, summer, spring: wind, rain, ice, fire. Now the cold was a tired old resident, always there, bored and heavy, lazy and indifferently spinning webs tinged with ice, stagnant, ever so content to stay put. Even when the wind was blowing through the apartment, blowing like in some classic Hollywood storm, the cold just sat there, not making a sound. It had permeated the plaster. It had sunk into the splintered red floors. It was wedged into the finest cracks in pipes, stone, and brick. It sat stupidly on the linoleum. It rested impressively on my desk. It embraced my books. It slept in my bed. It was like a great haze of light, a spectacular aura, around the coffeepot. It lay like a corpse in a bathtub. The cats hunched up in it, their coats wild and thick and standing on end, their eyes a little prehistoric and haunted. They tumbled together in it, touching it sometimes gingerly with humbly uplifted paws to see if it was real. Prowling or crouched and filled with disbelief, they sought to stumble on a pocket of air slightly heated by breath or accidental friction. There was no refuge of more than a few seconds' duration.

The fumes that polluted the apartment came through the walls like death might, transparent, spreading out, persistent, inescapable. A half mile down, five long flights, immigrants cooked greasy hamburgers for junkies, native-born. Each hamburger spit out particles of grease, smoke, oil, dirt, and each particle sprang wings and flew up toward heaven, where we tenement angels were. The carbon monoxide from incomplete combustion was a gaseous visitation that blurred vision, caused acute, incomprehensible pain inside the head, and made the stomach cringe in waiting vomit. The gas could pass through anything, and did: a clenched fist; layers of human fat; the porous walls of this particular slum dwelling; the human heart and brain and especially the abdomen, where it turned spikelike and tore into the lower intestine with sharp bitter thrusts. Molecules whirled in the wall: were the wall

100

itself whirling: wondrous: each molecule providing elaborate occasion for generous invasion: dizzying space for wandering stink and stench and poison. The wall simply ceased to be solid and instead moved like atoms under a microscope. I expected to be able to put my hand, gently, softly, kindly, through it. It would fade and part like wisps of cotton candy, not clinging even that much, or it would be like a film ghost: I would be able to move through it, it not me being unreal. The wall had become an illusion, a mere hallucination of the solid, a phantom, a chimera, an oasis born of delirium for the poor fool who thirsted for a home, shelter, a place inside not outside, place distinctly different from the cold streets of displacement and dispossession, a place barricaded from weather and wind and wet.

Each day—each and every day—I walked, six hours, eight hours, so as not to be poisoned and die. Each day there was no way to stay inside and also to breathe because the wind did not move the fumes any more than it moved the cold: both were permanent and penetrating, staining the lungs, bruising the eyes. Each day, no matter how cold or wet or ugly or dusty or hot or wretched, the windows were open and I walked: anywhere: no money so there was little rest: few stops: no bourgeois indulgences: just cement. And each night, I crawled back home, like a slug, dragging the day's fatigue behind me, dreading the cold open exposed night ahead. In my room, where I worked writing, the windows were never closed because the stench and poison were too thick, too choking. After midnight, I could close two windows in the living room just so no one went in it and just so they were open again by 6 am when the cooks heated up the grease to begin again. Sometimes, in my room, writing, my fingers were jammed stiff from the cold. Sometimes the typewriter rebelled, too cold to be pushed along. I found a small electric heater, and if I placed it just right, out of the wind but not so close to me that my clothes would burn, my fingers would regain feeling and they would begin to bend subtly and hit the right keys, clumsy, slow, but moving with deliberation. Less numbed, they moved, a slow dance of heroic movement: words on a page.

Each night, until dawn was finally accomplished, fully alive and splendid, I wrote, and then I would crawl, broken-hearted and afraid of dying, to one small distant room, the size of a large closet, where the fumes were less, and I would sleep on the floor on an old Salvation Army mattress with springs that some reformed alcoholic had never quite finished under an open window. I would dream: oh, Freud, tell me, what could it mean: of cold, of stench, of walking, of perhaps dying. Morbid violences and morbid defeats: cement, rain, wind, ice. Time would pass: I would tremble: I would wake up screaming: driven back to sleep to be warmer, I would dream of cold, of stench, of walking, of perhaps dying. Then, it would be time to wake up. I would be tired and trembling, so tired. I would walk, six hours, eight hours. After the first two winters I never got warm. Even in the hell of tenement heat, I never got warm. I dreaded cold like other people are afraid of being tortured: could they stand it, would they tell, would they beg, would they die first right away, struck down by dread, would they dirty their pants, would they beg and crawl. I wanted to surrender but no one would accept my confession and finish me off.

He kissed me against my will and then I walked home, slowly, in the rain, wet.

*

My love, the boy I lived with, lay sleeping, curled up in a ball, fetal, six feet, blond, muscled, and yet his knees were drawn up to his chest and his sweet yellow curls fell like a two-year-old's over his pale, drawn face, and his skin was nearly translucent, the color of ice spread out over great expanses of earth. He was dressed in layers of knitted wool, thermal pants and shirts, sweatshirts: we always wore all we had inside. The quilt with a wool blanket on top of it had shifted its place and his knees and face were brought together, his hands lost somewhere between them. I sat watching him, lost, in this room of his. He was on brown sheets. The radiator clanged and chugged: the noise it made was almost deafening, only in this room. There were big windows, and a fire escape splayed out under them going down to the treacherous street. There was a big desk buried under piles of papers. There were books, thrown, strewn, left for months open at one place so that the binding broke and the page itself seemed pressed to death.

There were books in all stages of being opened and closed with passages marked and pages bent and papers wedged into the seams of the binding with hand-scribbled notes, yellowing. The books were everywhere in great piles and clusters, under typewriter paper that simply spread like some wild growth in moist soil, under heaps of dirty clothes, under old newspapers that were now documents of an older time, under shoes and socks, under discarded belts, under old undershirts, under long-forgotten soda bottles not quite empty, under glasses ringed with wet, under magazines thrown aside in the second before sleep. Oh, my love could sleep. In the ice, in wind, in rain, in fire, my love could sleep. I watched him, content, a golden-haired child, some golden infant, peaceful, at ease in the world of coma and unremembered dreams. It was Christian sleep, we both agreed, mostly Protestant, impervious to guilt or worry or pain, Christ had died for him. To my outsider's eye it was grace. It soothed, it was succor, it was an adoring visitor, a faithful friend, it loved and rested him, and he knew no suffering that withstood its gentle solace. I had seen the same capacity for sleep in persons less kind, one was born to it, the great and deep and easy sleep reserved for those not meant to remember.

I sat on the other side of the room where he slept, in a typing chair bought in the cheapest five and dime, slightly built, perilous, covered in cat hair. His desk was huge, an old, used table, big enough to hold the confusion, which, regardless, simply billowed over its edges and onto the floor. The ground between the typing chair and his heavy, staid double bed was a false garden of tangle and weeds, or a minefield in the dark, but he slept with the light on, even he never quite safe because it was more like sleeping outside than sleeping inside. He would never be vagabonded: never desolate and out in the cold. But I would be, someday, putting on all the old trashy clothes, army surplus, of these cold years, walking forever, simply settling outside because inside was ridiculous, too silly, an insupportable idea: the absurd idea that this was a place to live. Sleep kept him believing he had a home—somewhere, after all, to sleep. But I spent the nights awake, I had to sit at a desk, turn on electric lights, refer to many different and highly important books, pace, sharpen pencils, change typewriter ribbons, make drafts, take notes, make phone calls, in mean-ingful and purposeful ways, with dignity and skill, physically inside, certainly inside. That old woman I would soon be, always outside, sat right near me, I could smell her savage skin, the mixture of sweat and ice, fear and filth. I already had her sores on my feet and her bitterness in my heart. I knew her: I was her already, carefully concealing it: waiting for the events between this moment and later when I would be her. My gray hair would hang from the dirty saliva in my mouth and I would push along some silly belongings: books no doubt, and some writings, and maybe a frazzled cat on a leash, because otherwise I would be desperately lonely. Between us, this old woman and me, there was just this sweet sleeping boy, a giant of pale beauty and barely conceivable kindness. He was at least slightly between her and me, and all my rush to despair was moderated by this small quiet miracle of our time together on earth. There was nothing perfect in it: but it was gentle: for me, the kindest love in a life of being loved too much. I sat in the typing chair, warmed by watching him sleep that foreign sleep of peace, I watched him and I believed in his peace and his rest: what was impossible he made real: and then his eyes fluttered open, and with so many different sounds in his voice, the whole range of calling and wanting, he called me: said my name, reached out, and I walked over and touched his hand: and he said, you're home, and he asked what was wrong.

And I raged. I bellowed. I howled. I was delirious with pain. I was shrill with humiliation. I was desperate with accusation and paranoid but defensible prophecy and acrid recrimination against what would happen to *me*. To *me*. The insufferable editor, the arrogance, the terms of the agreement: my fury, my rage, my memory of my life as a woman. Nearly keening in anguish, I told him about the café, the literature, the obsessed man, the kiss.

"You've done it before," he said quietly. And went back to sleep.

*

You know what I meant. This is the world you live in. You've done it before, he said. Oh, yes.

Shit you know what I meant.

You know what I meant.

I am trying to pace, windows open, under the weight of blankets. He is sitting up on his bed, under blankets.

You know what I meant.

Oh, I do.

Some things are true. What he meant is true. I know what, I know how, I know where, I know when, I even know why.

Oh, I do.

*

But I don't want to.

He says my name. Please, he says, wanting me to stop.

But really, I don't want to.

He says my name, pleading. Please, he says, please, I know, I know, but what can you do?

But I don't want to. I want, I say, I want, I say, to be this human being, and I want, I say, I want, to have somebody publish my book, I say, this simple thing, I say, I want, I want, I say, to be treated just like a human being, I say, and I don't want, I say, I don't want, I say, to have to do this. I have nowhere else to go, no one else who will do this simple thing, publish my book, but I don't want to have to do this.

He says my name, softly. Please, he says, please, stop, you must, he says, stop, because, he says, this is making me crazy, he says, softly he calls my name, please, he says, there is nothing to do, he says, calling my name softly and weeping, what is there to do, what can you do?

I want, I say, I want to be treated a certain way, I say. I want, I say, to be treated like a human being, I say, and he, weeping, calls my name, and says please, begging me in the silence not to say another word because his heart is tearing open, please, he says, calling my name. I want, I say, to be treated, I say, I want, I say, to be treated with respect, I say, as if, I say, I have, I say, a right, I say, to do what I want to do, I say, because, I say, I am smart, and I have written, and I am good, and I do good work, and I am a good writer, and I have published, and I want, I say, to be treated, I say, like someone, I say, like a human being, I say, who has done something, I say, like that, I say, not like a whore, not like a whore, I say, not any more, I say, and he says, calling my name, his tongue whispering my name, he says, calling my name and weeping, please, I know, I know. And I say to him, seriously, someday I will die from this, just from this, just from being treated like a whore, nothing else, I will die from it. And he says dryly, with a certain self-evident truth on his side: you will probably die from pneumonia actually. Ice hangs, ready to cut each chest. I hesitate, then crack up. We collapse, laughing. The blankets bury us alive.

*

He sleeps curled up blond, like a pale infant, in a room five floors above a desperate street corner. The windows are open, of course, and he sleeps, pale and dreamless, curled up and calm. The stairs outside his windows, rusty and fragile, go from our tenement heaven down to the grimmest cement. The sirens passing that corner blast the brick building, so that we might be in a war zone, each siren blast meaning we must get up and run to a shelter to hide. But there is no shelter. There is the occasional bomb by terrorist groups. Arson. Prostitutes. Pimps. Junkies. Old men, vagabonded, drunk with running sores, abscesses running obscene with green pus, curled up like my love, but blocking our doorway, on the front step, on the sidewalk under the step, behind the garbage cans, curled up just in the middle of the cement anywhere, just wherever they stopped. The blasts of the sirens go all day and all night and in between them huge buses make the building shake and wild taxis careen with screeching brakes. Cars rocket by, men with guns and clubs sounding their sirens, flashing lights that spread a fierce red glare into our little home: red flashing lights that climb five flights in the space of a second and illuminate us whatever we are doing, wherever we stand, in one second a whorish red, turn us and everything we see and touch into a grotesque special effect. Sirens that blare and blast and make the brick shake, announcing fire or murder or rape or a simple beating. Screams sometimes that come from over there, or behind that building, or in the courtyard, or some other apartment, or the nice man with the nice dog ranting at his mother over eighty and her screaming for help. Across the street there is a disco: parties for hire and music that makes the light fixtures quake between the siren blasts. Sometimes a flight above us, right near the roof, the filthy vagabonds sneak in and hide, piss and shit, urine runs down the hall stairs from the roof and a stench befouls even the awful air, and so cautiously the police are called, because the drunken, ruthless men might be armed, might hit, might rape: might kill.

The sirens blast the air, wind runs wild like plague through the rooms: and outside on the street men are curled up in fetal position, all hair and scabs and running sores, feet bandaged in newspaper and dirty torn cloth, eyes running pus, a bottle, sometimes broken to be used as a weapon, held close to the chest. The women on the great spiked heels, almost as cold as we are, can barely stand. They wobble from the fix, their shoulders hang down, their eyes hang down, their skin gets yellow or ochre, their faces are broken out in blotches, their hair is dry and dead and dirty, their knees buckle: they are too undressed for the cold: they can barely walk from the fix: they have broken teeth: they have bruises and scars and great running tracks: and all this they try to balance on four-inch, six-inch, heels; toe-dancers in the dance of death. On this corner mostly they are thin, too thin, hungered-away thin, smacked-away thin: thin and yellow.

In the park down at the end of the block, not far away, the drugs change hands. The police patrol the park: giving tickets to those who take their dogs off the leash. In the daylight, four boys steal money from an old man and run away, not too fast, why bother. The dealers sit and watch. The police stroll by as the deals are being made. Any dog off a leash is in for serious trouble.

Ambulances drag by. Cars hopped up sounding like a great wall falling flash by, sometimes crashing past a streetlight and bending it forever. Buses trudge with their normal human traffic. The cops coast by, sometimes with sirens, sometimes flashing red, just to get past the stoplight. Fire engines pass often, fast, serious, all siren and flashing light: this is serious. Arson. Bad electrical wiring. Old tenements, like flint. Building code violations. Whole buildings flame up. We see the fires, the smoke, the red lights. First we hear the sirens, see the flashing light with its crimson brilliance, then we ask, is it here, is it us? We make jokes: that would warm us up. Where are the cats? Can we get them out in time? We have a plan, a cage we can pull down from a storage place (we have no closets, only planks scattered above our heads, hanging on to the edges of walls), and then we can rush them all in and rush out and get away: to where? He sleeps. How?

On TV news we see that in New York City where we live people die from the cold each winter. We have called and written every department of the city. We have withheld rent. We have sued. No one cares. We know that we could die from the cold. But fire—they must care about fire, they have a fire department, we see the fire engines and the flashing red lights and we hear the sirens. No cold department, no whore department, no vagabond department, no running-pus-and-sores department, no get-rid-of-the-drug-dealers department: but fire and dogs-on-the-leash departments seem to abound. I am always pleasantly surprised that they care about fire.

The disco music is so loud that we cannot hear our own radio: we call the police. There is an environmental-something department. They will drive by and measure the decibel level of the sound. This is a great relief. Can someone come and take the temperature in our apartment? The policeman hangs up. A crank call, he must think, and what with so many real problems, so much real violence, so many real people dying. My pale blond friend sleeps, his skin bluish. I call the police about the noise.

The landlord has installed a lock on our building. The lock must be nearly unique. You turn it with a key and when you hear a certain click you must at that second push open the door. If you miss the click you must start all over again. If your key goes past the click, the door stays locked and you must complete the cycle, complete the turn, before you can start again, so it takes even longer, and if you miss it again you must still keep going: you must pay attention and put your ear right up against the lock to hear the click. The fetal vagabonds run pus at your feet and the drooping prostitutes come at you, perhaps wanting one second of steadiness on their feet or perhaps wanting to tear out your heart, and this is a place where men follow women with serious expectations not to be trifled with, pursue in cars, beep from cars, follow block after block in cars, carry weapons, sneak up behind, rob, need money, need dope, and you must stand there at exquisite attention and listen for the little click.

The cement on the corner has been stained by its human

trash: it is the color of a hundred dead junkies somehow ground into the stone, paved smooth, running like mud in the rare moonlight. Sometimes there is blood, and sometimes a savage dog, belonging to one of the drunken men, chases you and threatens to tear you apart and in terror you edge your way inside: listening carefully for the little click. In a great urban joke, God has given us all the trappings of a civilized society. We have a huge intersection with a traffic light. We have a bus stop. Across the street there is a bank and a school as well as a disco. Next door there is a large church with stained glass and ornate and graceful stonework. The intersection has the bank, a hospital diagonal from us, and a fast-food chicken place. And then, resting right next to us, right under us, tucked near, is the home of the hamburger itself, the great gift of this country, right on our corner, with its ascending ordure. I laugh frequently. I am God's best fan.

*

The windows are open, of course, and he sleeps, pale and dreamless, curled up and calm, nearly warm except that his skin has become a pale blue, barely attached to the fine bones underneath. Outside the sirens blast the brick building, they almost never stop. Fire and murder. Cars rocketing by, men with guns and clubs and flashing lights that climb five flights in the space of a second and turn us whorish red, like great wax museum freaks in a light show.

I listen to the music from the disco, which is so loud that the Mozart on my poor little $32 radio is drowned out. Tonight, perhaps, is the Italian wedding, and so we have an imitator of Jerry Vale to a disco beat that carries across the wide street, through air freighted with other weight, screams and blasts, and into the epicenter of my brain. If I close the windows, however, I will probably die. But it is the vibration, in this case the endless clucky thumping of the badly abused instruments, that worms its way under my skin to make me itch with discontent, irritation, a rage directed, in this case, at Italian weddings, but on other nights at French crooners, at Jaggerish deadbeats, at Elvisian charlatans, at Haggardish kvetchers, and even, on occasion, at Patti Pageish or even Peggy Leeish dollies embellished by brass.

I watch the limos pulling up, parking in front of the fire

hydrants and no-parking signs. I see a man in a tux tear down
with his bare hands a no-parking sign. I see an endless supply
of kids attending these adult parties. The house used to be a
synagogue. One day it was empty. Then a man with many
boys moved in. The boys had tattoos and did heavy work and
had lean thighs. They all lived on the top floor. The parties
were on the lower two floors. The boys flew a flag from the
top floor. I called it never-never-land. The parties drove me
mad.

The women who went into the house were never contem-
porary cosmopolitan women. They always wore fluffy dresses
or full skirts and frilly blouses, very fifties, suburban, dating,
heavy makeup. Even the youngest women wore wide formal
skirts, maybe even with crinolines, in pastel colors, and their
hair was set and lacquered. They were deferential and flirty
and girlish and spoke when spoken to. Sometimes they had a
corsage. Sometimes they wore female hats. Sometimes they
even wore female gloves or female wraps. Always they wore
female shoes and female stockings and stood in a female way
and looked very fifties, virgin ingenues. They never met the
rough boys from the top floor, or not so that I could see. They
came with dates. There were floral arrangements inside, and
white tablecloths, and men in white jackets. Then, during the
day, the boys from the upper floor would ride their bikes or
get wrecked on drugs. Once my favorite, a beautiful wrecked
child who at fifteen was getting old, too covered with tattoos,
with hair hanging down to his shoulders and some beautiful
light in his eyes and thighs, had a young girl there. She too was
beautiful, dark, perfect, naked, exquisite breasts and thighs,
they hung out the window together and watched the sun rise.
They seemed exquisitely happy: young: not too hurt yet, or
young enough to be resilient: he must have been hurt, all
tattooed and drugged out and in this house of boys, and she
had been or would be, and I prayed for her as hard as I have
ever hoped for myself. That she was and would be happy; that
she was older than she looked; that she would be all right. It
was only at dawn that the human blood seemed to have washed
out of the cement and that injury seemed to disappear: and
men began emerging from the park where they had been
fucking and sucking cock all night: they were weary and at

peace: and there seemed to be a truce just then, for the duration of the dawn, between night and day, between people and despair. The boy and girl, radiant and tender with pleasure, hung out of the window. Underneath them men dragged themselves toward home, tender with fatigue. I sat by the open window and smiled. It was the only time to be awake and alive on that Lower East Side street corner. The light would be not quite daylight: night was still mixed in with it: and there was peace. Then the sun would be up, glaring and rude. The night would be defeated and angry, preparing to return with a vengeance. The vagabonds would shit and move. The fumes would begin anew for the day, inevitably thicker and more repellent than before, more repulsive than it was possible to be or to imagine or to engineer or to invent. The whores would go home short and lose more teeth. The boys across the way would shoot up, sleep, eventually ride their bikes or go stand on street corners. I would go to the small distant room and try to sleep on the Salvation Army mattress under the open window. I would hear the sirens. I would wake up burning, with ice not fire.

*

I would sit by the open windows in the living room and watch the dark, then the light: dawn was my pleasure, a process pungent with melodrama, one thickness edging out another, invading it, permeating it: dark being edged out, a light weighing the night down until it was buried in the cement. You could slice the night and you could slice the day, and it was just the hour or two, some parts of the year it seemed like only minutes, in which both mixed together resembling peace. The light would begin subtly and I could just see some treetops up the street in the park. At first they looked like a line, a single line, an edge of jagged mountaintops etched against a dark eternity with a sharp, slight pencil, and gradually the line filled in, got deeper and deeper until the shape of each tree got filled in, and then color came, the brown branch, bare, the leaf-covered branch, green, the blossom-covered branch, chartreuse. I could see some dogs being walked early, the first ones of the day coming, forms under artificial light turning into creatures of flesh and blood when the real light came. I could see, in the next room, the tousled head of my love, the boy I live with, sleeping. Soon he would wake up and I would go to sleep and he would go to work and I would have stopped working: now while he still slept and I was a vigilant consciousness I opened the windows that had been closed in the living room and sat down next to them to watch the dawn, the kindest time.

In the hour before my turn came, my turn to sleep, night would brand me: it would go through my brain, and make pictures there of itself: every figure of horror would escape the night and enter my brain: and each mundane piece of a living day, the coming light, would grow huge and induce fear: a drip under the sink was a torrent, irresolvable, menacing: so there was no time to sleep: and the plaster falling from the ceiling would become the promised disaster: and there was no time to sleep: and the crack in the toilet threatened sewage and flood: and so, it was impossible to sleep: and there was the landlord to be called, and the windows were open, and congestion in the chest, and shopping to do, and noises on the roof, and some strange sounds from below: and so it was impossible to sleep. The drip under the sink would mean calling the super: and this meant no sleep: because he was a small, mean, angry man, aloof but radiating hot cruelty, one little man knotted into one fist of a man. His wife, having no English, would answer the phone and in terror stammer out "asleep" or "not here" or "no, no." Once she begged me in splatters of languages I did not speak: do not make me get him, miss, he will hurt me. The sink would be stopped up beyond help, or there would be no heat or no hot water, for us in this cold place a disaster of unparalleled dimensions, and she would whisper in chokes: do not make me get him, miss, he will hurt me. I knew the sound of the swollen larynx waiting to burst.

The day would be solidly established, that graceless light, and the people of the day would begin moving on the street, the buses would come one after another, the traffic would rev up for the day ahead, the smoke from all the motor engines would begin escalating up, the noise would become fearsome, the chatter from the street would become loud and busy, the click click click of shoes and boots would swallow up the cement, the voices would become various and in many languages: and I would make my way down the hall to the small room with the broken springs in the mattress under the open window and try to sleep.

I dreamed, for instance, of being in a tropical place. It was all green, that same steady bright unchanging green under too much light that one finds in the steamy tropics, that too-lush green that hurts the eyes with its awful brightness, only it was duller because it seemed to know it was in a dream. And in the steaming heat of this too-green jungle with its long thin sharp leaves and branches resembling each other, more like hungry animals than plants, stretched out sideways not up, growing out wide not up, but still taller than me, there was a clearing, a sort of burnt-out, brown-yellow clearing, short grass, flat, a circle surrounded by the wild green bush. There were chairs, like the kinds used in auditoriums, folding chairs set up, about eight of them in a circle like for a consciousness-raising group or a small seminar. The sun burned down. I was standing. Others were sitting in the chairs, easy, relaxed, men and women, I knew them but I don't know who they were by name, now or then, and I have a big knife, a huge sharp knife, and very slowly I walked up to the first one and I slowly slit her throat. No one moves or notices and I walk to the next one and I slit her throat, and I walk to the next one and I slit his throat, and slowly I walked around the circle of sitting people and I slit each throat slowly and purposefully. I wake up shaking and screaming, burning hot, in terror. In the dream I was truly happy.

Or I dream the dream I hate most, that I am awake, I see the room, someone is in it, I hear him, he has a knife, I wake up, I try to scream, I can't scream, I am awake, I believe I am awake, but I cannot scream and I cannot move, my eyes are open, I can see and hear everything but I cannot do anything, I keep trying to scream but I make no sound, I cannot move, so I think I must not be awake, and I force myself to wake up and it turns out that I wasn't awake before but I am now, and I hear the man in the room, and I can see him moving around, and I am awake, and I try to scream but no sound comes out and I try to move but I cannot move, but I am awake, and I see everything and I hear everything, every detail of the room I know I am in, every sound that I know is there, every detail of reality, the time, the sounds of the neighbors, I know where I am and who I am and that I am awake and still I can't say anything, I try to scream but I can't, the vocal cords do not work, the voice does not work, my mouth works but no sound comes out, and I try to force myself to get up but my body does not move, and then I realize that even though I think I am awake I must not be awake and so I force myself to wake up, I fight and I fight to wake up, and then I wake up, and I hear the man in the room, I see him, I see his face, I see him and see every detail of who he is and how he is dressed and how he moves and where he goes and I see myself and I know I am in bed and he is in the room and I hear every sound and I try to scream but I cannot and I try to move but I cannot and so I try to force myself again to wake because I know I must be asleep and I am so terrified I cannot move from fear and I cannot scream from fear: and by the time I wake up I am half dead. Drenched in sweat, I try to sleep some more.

I hear my love, my friend, moving around, awake, alive. I am relieved. The night is over. I can begin to try to sleep. I hear him turn on the water, he is there if it floods. I have left him a note, probably two pages long, filled with worries and admonitions: what must be done to get through this day coming up, the vivid imperatives that came to press in on my brain as night ended and I knew I would have to sleep, the dread demands of uncompromising daylight: more calls to the city, more calls to the landlord, more calls to the lawyers, more calls to the super: and buy cat litter: and remember the laundry, to take it in or to pick it up and I have left money, five dollars: and I love you, have a good day, I hope it goes well. I can't sleep in his bed because in the day his room has fumes, even with the windows open. So I am down in this little closet under an open window to sleep. Somehow my friend comes home at night, it is a surprise always, and I am always, inevitably, without fail, a cold coiled spring ready to snap and kill, a minefield of small, deadly explosions. Dinner is eaten in front of partially opened windows. I cannot live through this one more day, I say, each and every night, sometimes trying to smile and be pleasant, sometimes my face twisted in grief or rage. I am going to: kill the landlord. Today I almost threw a rock through the windows of the hamburger place. Today I almost went up to the man who runs it and spit at

him, hit him, cursed him, called him foul names, threw myself
on him and tore his throat open. All day long, every minute of
every day, but especially today, whichever day it is, I want to
kill, burn down, tear down, destroy, put an end to this,
somehow, anyhow. He does the dishes. I stalk him. I want to
talk with you, I want an answer, what are we going to do,
where are we going to go, I want to move to a hotel, I want to
move, I want to leave this city, I am going to kill somebody, I
want the landlord to die, I want to slice out his heart, I want
to pound him into the ground myself, these hands, I am going
to call him now and tell him what a foul fuck he is, what a
pig, I am going to threaten him, his wife, his children, I am
going to make them as afraid as I am cold, I know we don't
have any money but I have to go to a hotel I can't stay here I
am going to burn down the restaurant I know how to make
bombs I am going to bomb it I am going to pour sand down
their chimney I am going to throw rocks I am going to burst
the windows I am going to explode it and break all the glass I
am going to set a fire I am going to smash my fists through the
windows. I almost did that tonight, he says, shaking, I almost
couldn't stop myself, I almost broke all the windows. I am
quiet. He is gentle, I am the time bomb. I look at him. He is all
turned inward with pain, on the edge of a great violence which
we are united in finding unspeakable when it comes from him:
we are believers in his tenderness: it is our common faith. He
has a surface, calm and clear as a windless, warless night:
underneath perhaps he too is cold, or perhaps I am simply
driving him mad. He wants to throw rocks, not egged on by
me but when alone, coming home. He cannot bear violence, in
himself, near him. I have absorbed it endlessly, I can withstand
anything. I am determined to keep calm, I see I am hurting
him with my bitter invective, I am determined to get through
another night, another day. He reads. Perhaps he is cold too?
We talk. We touch hands quietly. We fall asleep together in his
bed marooned. I wake up soon. He is asleep, curled up like a
lamb of peace. Perhaps you have never known a gentle man.
He is always a stranger, unarmed, at night wrapped in simple
sleep he curls up like a child in someone's arms. It is after 11
pm, the restaurant has now been closed long enough for the
wind streaming through the apartment to have cleared out my

room so that I will not choke or get head pain or throw up or have sharp pains in my gut. My lungs will ache from the cold. My fingers will be stiff. My throat will hurt from the cold. I sit down to work. I must write my book. I work until the dawn, my salvation, day after day, when I see the beauty of earth unfolding. I watch dawn come on the cement which is this earth of mine. Then I sleep my kind of sleep, of cold and burning, of murder and death, of paralysis and silent screams, of a man with a knife who moves with impunity through a consciousness tortured with itself, of the throats I have slit, of the heat of that tropical place. In the dream there was no blood but I wake up knowing that it must have been terrible, smelly and heavy and sticking and rotting fast in the sun.

*

I watch him sleep because the tenderness I have for him is what I have left of everything I started with.

My brother was like him, frail blond curls framing a guileless face, he slept the same way, back where I started. A tenderness remembered tangentially, revived when I see this pale, yellow-haired man asleep, at rest, defenseless, incomprehensibly trusting death not to come. We are innocence together, before life set in.

Sometimes I feel the tenderness for this man now, the real one asleep, not the memory of the baby brother—sometimes I feel the tenderness so acutely—it balances on just a sliver of memory—I feel it so acutely, it is so much closer to pain than to pleasure or any other thing, for instance, in one second when each knows what the other will say or without a thought our fingers just barely touch, I remember then in a sharp sliver of penetration my baby brother, pale, yellow-haired, curls framing a sleeping face while I lay awake during the long nights, one after the other, while mother lay dying. It is consumingly physical, not to sleep, to be awake, watching a blond boy sleeping and waiting for your mother to die. Or I remember my brother, so little, just in one second, all joy, a tickle-fight, we are squared off, each in a corner of the sofa (am I wearing my cowgirl outfit with gun and holster?), father is the referee, and we are torrents of laughter, rapturous wrestling, and his curly yellow hair cascades. He was radiant with delight, lit up from inside, laughing in torrents and me too. My childhood was this golden thing, eradicable, intense sensations of entirely physical love remembered like short, sweet, delirious hallucinations, lucid in fog. Now I love no one, except that tender man now in the next room dreaming without memory, a blessed thing, or not dreaming at all: that curled-up blond muscled thing recalling every miracle of love from long ago. I was happy then: don't dare deny it.

I don't love now, at all, except when I remember to love the blond boy, the stranger not even related to me, not part of anything from before, who sleeps in the next room: a tall blond man: when I remember to love him certain minutes of certain days. Don't look for my heart. The beasts have eaten it. What is his name?

> Our women writers write like women writers,
> that is to say, intelligently and pleasantly,
> but they are in a terrible hurry to tell what
> is in their hearts. Can you explain why a
> woman writer is never a serious artist?
>
> Dostoyevsky

*

I came back from Europe. I lived alone in a pink apartment on the Lower East Side across from the police precinct. I wanted to be a writer. I want to write. Every day I write. I am alone and astonishingly happy.

The police cars ram into the crushed sidewalk across the street. The precinct is there. Men in blue with guns and nightsticks swarm. Garbled sounds emanate from radios on their hips. They swarm outside the impressive stone building, the precinct headquarters. Red lights flash. A dozen cars swerve in or swerve out, crash in or crash out, are coming or going, burning rubber on the burning streets, the smell of the burnt rubber outlasting the sound of the siren as its shrillness fades.

The police cars never slow down. They stop immediately. They start up at once, no cautionary note, the engine warming. They pull straight out at top speeds or swerve in and almost bang against the building but somehow the brake gets the weight of the cop and the sidewalk is crushed on its outer edge.

The sirens blare day and night. The cars bump and grind and flash by, day and night. The blue soldiers mass like ants, then deploy, day and night. The red of the flashing lights illuminates my room, like a scarlet searchlight, day and night.

The police are at war with the Hell's Angels, two blocks away. The motorcycles would collect. The swastikas would be emblazoned, the leather would defy the summer heat, the chains would bang like drums through the always-percussive air hitting the cement. You could hear the anguish of the motorcycles, hear the anguish of the streets, as the burning rubber scarred them: the police cars would pull out fast and there would be a din of dull anguish sounding like distant war, there would be the pain of acute exploding sounds that made the buildings move and shake and your body was shocked by it even before your mind could understand that you had not been killed. There were fires too, loud red fire trucks: real fire, the building across the street next to the precinct building burning, the top two floors burning, the building right next to mine burning. The red lights would flash like great red searchlights and the sirens would scream right into the blood: and there would be fire.

Across from the precinct in a gravel lot the police parked their regular civilian cars and boys played basketball.

The street seemed to be overrun with uniforms, fires, guns, cars careening in and out. The red searchlights and sirens made it seem that the Martians had landed, or the army, or war had come, or giant insects, or man-eating plants. Each day was a surreal drama, an astonishment of military noise and civic emergency.

It was not the usual exile of the Lower East Side: condemned into a circle of hell from which there was no exit, no one ever left alive, no sign anywhere of what others call "the social order"; instead, the social order swarmed and crushed side-walks, was martial and armed; the social order put out fires that continued to burn anyway from one building to the next, flaring up here, flaring up there, like one continuous fire, teasing, teasing the men with the great hoses and the heroic helmets. It was not the usual Lower East Side exile: one was not marooned forever until death with only seawater to put to one's parched and broken lips: one could scream and maybe someone with boots and a gun and a uniform and a right to kill would take time out from the military maneuvers of the swarming militia and keep one from becoming a corpse. One hoped, but not really, that a single woman's scream might be heard over the military din. Right next to the precinct, in the building next door, a burglar crawled into the apartment of a woman in broad daylight, the middle of the hot afternoon, simply by bending the cheap gate over her fire escape window and climbing in the open window. The army did not stop him. When he set the fire that killed her as she napped that after-noon, the red searchlights did not find him; the sirens, the hoses, the trucks, the helmets, did not deter him.

*

The apartment was five flights up. The numbering of the floors was European. The ground floor was not the first floor, it had no number. The first floor was up a steep flight of stairs. The fifth floor was at the top of a huge climb, a mountain of stone steps, a hiker's climb up. It was not too far from God. Each day an old, old, heavy Ukrainian woman, bent, covered in heavy layers of black skirts and black shawls, black scarf tied tight around her head hiding her hair except for white wisps, washed the stairs, bottom to top, then cleaned the banisters, top to bottom. She had her bucket and a great mop of stringy ropelike mess, and a pile of rags: stoop-shouldered she washed and rinsed, washed and rinsed, dusted and polished. There was no smell of urine. In each hall there were three toilets, one for each apartment on the floor. The toilet was set in concrete. The cubicle was tiny. It didn't lock from the outside, but there was a hook on the inside. Each tenant cleaned their own.

The apartment was newly painted, a bright Mediterranean pink, fresh, garish, powdery. You walked in right to the kitchen, there was no subtle introduction, it was splintered, painted wood floors, no distinct color, a radiator, a grotesque, mammoth old refrigerator with almost no actual space inside, a tiny stove, and a bathtub. There was a window that opened onto a sliver of an airshaft. There was a room on either side of the kitchen. To the left, on the street, above the teeming blue soldiers and desperate fire trucks, there was a living room, small but not tiny. It had a cockroach-ridden desk, one straight-backed wooden chair, and I bought a $12 piece of foam rubber to sleep on, cut to be a single mattress. I bought a bright red rug with a huge flower on it from Woolworth's, and laid it down like it was gold. Under it was old linoleum, creased, chunky, bloating. There were two windows, one opening onto the fire escape, I couldn't afford a gate and so it had to stay closed, and the other I risked opening. I found a small, beautiful bookcase, wood with some gracious curves as ornament, and in it I put like a pledge the few books I had carried across the ocean as talismans. The room to the right of the kitchen, covered in the same cracked linoleum, was like a small closet. The window opened on the airshaft, no air, just a triangular space near a closed triangle of concrete wall. The room was stagnant, the linoleum ghastly with old dirt ground into the cracks. The room was smothering and wretched. The walls sweated. I didn't go into it.

The toilet in the hall was outside the locks on the apartment door, outside the huge steel police lock, a steel pole that shored up the door in case of a ramming attack, outside the cylinder locks, outside the chain lock. I carried a knife back and forth and I slept with a knife under my pillow.

The glare of the lightbulbs was naked. The pink paint flaked and rubbed off to the naked touch. The heat enveloped one, the skin burned from the hot water in the air. I immersed myself in the bathtub: in the heat one never got dry: and lived between the desk and the mattress on the floor: writing and sleeping: concentrating: smiling at the red rug with the big flower. I learned to be alone.

*

The apartment was painted Mediterranean pink, the paint was powdery, I found some remnants of cheap cotton in a textile store and tacked them up over the windows: light came in unimpeded, the heat of the burning sun, the red searchlights of the military, the red alarm of fire, danger, must run, must escape, will burn. The walls between the apartments were thin. There was a thin wall between me and the man in the next apartment, a tiny man of timid gentleness. I heard long conversations and deep breaths, discussions about the seasoning in soups and the politics of anal warts, both subjects of his expertise. At night I would dream that there was a hole in the wall, and everything was like a play, the extended conversations, a two-person domestic drama: I knew I was sleeping but I believed the hole was real: and I knew I was sleeping but the conversations must have been real, in their real voices with their real inflections, as they sat there in my view. We had no secrets and at night when I would scream out in terror at a bad dream, I would alarm my neighbor, and the next day he would ask me if anyone had hurt me: late, timid. Above me the man would get fucked hard in the ass, as his expletives and explications and supplications and imperious pleadings would make clear. The two male bodies would thump on the floor like great stones being dropped over and over again, like dead weight dropping. Sleep could not intervene here and mask the sound for me in flashy narratives of story-within-the-story, play-within-the-play: the screams were too familiar, too close, not yet lost in life rushing forward.

I slept when I was tired. I wrote. Sweat poured out. I took long walks. My dreams were like delirium. I did not have hours or days. I simply went on. There was a great, soft stream of solitude and concentration and long, wet baths, and timid trips to the toilet. Oh, yes, I had a terrible time getting money and I don't want to say how I did it. I lived from day to day, stopping just short of the fuck. I had odd jobs. I did what was necessary. I was always happy when I was alone: except when restlessness would come like a robber: then I would walk, walk.

*

The pink walls and the red carpet with the huge flower were my indulgences. The rest was austere, the heat prohibiting excess, poverty offended by it. The single mattress was like a prayer.

I came alive again: in solitude: concentrating: writing.

*

Yes, there were men and women, women and men, but they were faded: they were background, not foreground, intrusions, failures of faith, laziness of spirit: forays into the increasingly foreign world of the social human being: they were brief piercing moments of sensation, the sensation pale no matter how acute, sentimental no matter how tough: namby-pamby silliness of thighs that had to open: narrow pleasure with no mystery, no subtlety, no subtext: pierce, come; suck, come; foretold pleasures contained between the legs, while solitude promised immersion, drenching, the body overcome by the radical intensity of enduring.

*

I met my beautiful boy, my lost brother, around, somewhere, and invited him in. I saw him around, here and there, and invited him in. Talking with him was different from anything else: the way the wind whispers through the tops of trees just brushed by sunset. It made me happy. I invited him in. My privacy included him. My solitude was not betrayed. We were like women together on that narrow piece of foam rubber, and he, astonished by the sensuality of it, ongoing, the thick sweetness of it, came so many times, like a woman: and me too: over and over: like one massive, perpetually knotted and moving creature, the same intense orgasms, no drifting separateness of the mind or fragmented fetishizing of the body: instead a magnificent cresting, the way a wave rises to a height pushing forward and pulls back underneath itself toward drowning at the same time: one wave lasting forever, rising, pulling, drowning, dying, all in the same movement; or a wave in an ocean of waves covering nearly all the earth, immense. My lost brother and I became lovers forever, buried there, in that sea so awesome in its density and splendor. I need never touch him again. He became my lover forever. So he entered my privacy, never offending it.

*

I had learned solitude, and now I learned this.

*

On his birthday I gave him a cat that had his face.

I had looked everywhere for it. I had looked in stores, I had traced ads, read bulletin boards, made phone calls. I had gone out, into the homes of strangers, looking for the cat I would know the minute I saw it. Red. With his face: a certain look, like a child before greed sets in, delicate, alert, listening. The day came and I didn't have it. I knew the cat was somewhere waiting, but I was afraid I would not find it. The day of his birthday I went out, looking, a last search, asking, following every lead, hour after hour. The heat was rancid. Then a man told me where to look: a woman had found a pregnant cat in a garbage dump and had taken it home: the kittens were red. He called her. I went there. The skies had darkened, gotten black. The air was dusty. The thunder cracked the cement. Hail fell. I ran to her house, awed by this surfeit of signs, afraid of the stones of ice and the black sky. In the house the cat with his face was waiting. I took the cat home.

*

Year after year, he is with me. Solitude is with me and he is with me. Now I've spent ten years writing. Imagine a huge stone and you have only your own fingernail. You scratch the message you must write into the stone bit by bit. You don't know why you must but you must. You scratch, one can barely see the marks, you scratch until the nail is torn and disintegrates, itself pulverized into invisible dust. You use the blood from your ripped finger, hoarding it to go on as long as you can but hurrying because you will run out. Imagine ten years of it. But the solitude changes. At first it is fresh and new, like any lover, an adventure, a ravishing excitement, a sensual derangement: then it gets deeper, tougher, lonelier, not because one wants the closeness of friends but because one doesn't, can't: can barely remember wanting anything but solitude. One remembers wanting, needing, like one remembers a childhood dream: but even the memory seems frivolous, trivial, a distraction: solitude kills the need for anything but itself, like any grand passion. It changes one, irrevocably. Promiscuous warmth dies, all goodhearted fellowship with others dies, seems false and cheap. Only burning ice is left inside. Whoever gets too near gets their skin burned off and dies from the cold.

He lives inside my privacy. He coexists with my solitude, hating it sometimes but rebelling in silence by himself because he does not want to leave: I would make him leave, even now. I put solitude first, before him. His complaints are occasional, muted. I keep him far away even when he is gentle, asleep, curled up next to me like an innocent child, my solace, my human heart. The years of solitude—the seconds, the minutes, the hours, night into morning, evening into night, day stretching into night and weeks stretching into months—are a moat he cannot cross. The years of being together with him—the seconds, the minutes, the hours, the days into weeks into months into years—do not change this. This is the way I love now.

You are nomads together, in cheap room after cheap room: poorer and poorer: the written word does not sell: some is published but it is not embraced, it offends, it does not make money, no one wants more of it, it has an odor, those with good taste demur: the pink apartment with the toilet in the hall is left behind: food stamps, bare foam rubber mattress that starts shredding and has great potholes like city streets, cold floors, cheap motels, the backs of rented trucks moving your few belongings from one shabby empty place to another: writing: hungry. He is closest and dear, loved more now, but he is necessarily outside the concentration and the pain of the task itself, the discipline and despair, the transcendent pleasure, the incommunicable joy. The writing makes one poorer and poorer: no one likes it. It gets worse and worse, over years, that is the hard part, over years, day by day, for years. One absorbs that too, endures it, getting dead and mutilated inside: one endures the continuing, worsening poverty and the public disgrace: strangers despise you, for what you think or what you write, or no one knows you. And you put writing, solitude, this failure, first, before him: and his way of loving you is not to take offense: not to point out the arrogant stupidity of the choice: but to stay, to let you leave him out, far away, in the chill region because you have a cold and awful heart. He is for human times. But writing is cold and alone. It makes you monstrous, hard, icy, colder and more barren, more ruthless, than the Arctic Sea.

*

Each book makes you poorer: not just blood: money, food, shelter: the more time you use writing but not making money, the poorer you are. Each book makes you poorer. You are awash in pain, the physical poverty, the inner desolation. You get deader and deader inside. The blood still stains the stone, a delicate pink, tiny drops rubbed into signs and gestures. The glacier moves slowly over the fertile plain, killing. Everything around you begins to die.

*

Solitude is your refuge and your tomb, where you are buried alive. Writing is your slow, inexorable suicide. Poverty is the day grinding into night, night hurling you back without mercy to day: day is teeth grinding to the exposed, raw nerves, slow, a torture of enduring. There are no human witnesses, only the lost boy asleep. He is tangled in knots of helpless rage. He thought life was fairer. He sleeps like a lost child. You are in a fever of creation, waiting to die, hurrying to finish first. There is more to do.

*

Solitude is a shroud, the creature inside it still alive; writing resistance to being bound up and thrown in a hole in the ground; poverty the wild weeds growing over the hard, lonely earth. The lost boy sleeps, breathes, suffers: fingernails scratching against the looking glass trying to get through, he can't bring Alice back.

*

Solitude is revenge. Writing is revenge. Poverty is your wild pride, open sores, matted hair, gorgon, rags, hairshirt, filth and smell: arrogant saint nailed to a tired old cross. He tells you he hates your pride. He does hate it.

*

It is too easy to be martyred. Your pride is more terrible than that. You keep fighting. Solitude is revenge. Writing is revenge. Medea, not Christ, is your model. Where are the children to kill? I could, I could. "I too can stab," she told Jason. I too can stab.

*

So now we have come to rest in this awful place, the windows open in the cold storm of winter, the fumes turning even the coldest, fiercest wind stagnant, rancid. The vagabonds shit in the foyer of the building's lobby and behind the stairwell and hide out on the landing above us. We are five flights up. There is no money to move one more time: and my friend, my sweet boy, sleeps in wool and thermal underwear and sweatshirts pale and blue as if frozen by death: and I sit by the open window in the dead of winter, wintry winter, the wind streaming in, a small electric heater just keeping my fingers from freezing up stiff, and I write, I am cold and tired beyond anything I can say, any words there are: a dying bird, broken wing, on a plain of ice; some creature, lost and broken, on a plain of ice, isolated, silent, fatigued, famished for warmth and rest and rescue, having no hope, wanting not to turn canni-bal before dying: crawling, crawling, trying to find the end of the icy plain, the rich brown earth, a plant, a flower: rescue, escape: some oasis not ruined by heavy, wet, implacable cold.

I am cold all the time. I walk six hours a day, eight hours a day, then come to this apartment where the windows are never closed. I am desperate beyond any imagining. You will never know. It is amazing that I do not kill.

*

I am afraid of dying, especially of pneumonia. I am sick all the time, fever, sore throat, chill to the bones, joints stiff, abdo-minal pains from the fumes, headaches from the fumes, diz-ziness from the fumes. I am afraid of sleeping, afraid of dying: each day is a nightmare of miles to walk not to die: is there money for a cup of coffee today? I am a refugee: profoundly despondent and tired enough to die: I want somewhere to live: really live: I imagine it: warm and pretty: clean: no human shit in piles: little bourgeois dreamer: dumb cunt: eyes hurt like Spinoza's: I am in the apartment, there is a driving rain, violent wind, I stand in the rain inside, drenched.

*

The fumes start in winter. Winter, spring, summer, fall, winter again, summer again: the edge of fall. The chill is in the marrow of the bones. The fatigue makes the eyes gray and yellow, great rings circle them: the skin is dirty ivory like soap left in a bathtub for years: the fatigue is like the awful air that rises from a garbage can left to melt in the sun: the fatigue especially sits on the tongue, slowing it down, words are said in broken syllables, sentences rarely finished: speech becomes desperate and too hard: the fatigue drowns the brain in sludge, there is no electricity, only the brain sinking under the weight of the pollution: the fatigue is smeared all over, inside the head it is in small lakes, and behind the eyes it drips, drips. It is fall. The windows are open. The book has been finished now. Many publishers have refused to publish it. There is virtually no one left to despise it, insult it, malign it, refuse it: and yet I have been refining it, each and every night, writing until dawn. Now I am tired and the book is perfect and I am done, a giant slug, a glob of goo. A woman lets me go to her apartment, on the ocean. Perhaps she saves my life.

*

In the living room there are large windows, and right outside them there is the beach, the ocean, the sky, the moon: the sound of the waves, the sound of the ocean moving over the earth becomes the sound of one's own breathing. It is foggy, hot, moist, damp, and when fog rises on the water, huge roaches climb the walls and rest on the tops of the windows. They are slow, covered in the sea mist, prehistoric, like the ocean itself. They seem part of my delirium, a fever of fatigue: I am alternately shivering, shaking delirious and comatose, almost dead: a corpse, staring, no pennies for her eyes. I have no speech left. I sit and stare, or shake and cry: but still, the ocean is there. I hear the ocean, I see the ocean: I watch the huge bugs: at dawn, I swim: I see the red sun rise and I swim: I hear the ocean, I watch the ocean, I see how it endures, going on and on, I listen to the sound of its endurance, I sit and stare or I shake, fevered. The bright sunlight breaks up the fog, dries up the mist, the huge brown bugs disappear: outside normal people chatter: the afternoons are long, dull, too much sun, too many chattering vulgar souls not destroyed, normal people with normal concerns: cheery seaside banter: old women on benches on the boardwalk right under my window: and at night teenagers drinking beer, listening to the blaring radios, courting, smoking. I avoid the bright sun of the afternoon and the normal people. I sit in the living room, the sound of the ocean cradles and rocks me, and I read Thomas Mann, listen to Mozart. When the vulgar afternoon is over, I watch the ocean and I listen to it endure. At night, I go out and in, out and in, walk the beach, walk the boardwalk, sit in the sand, the wet sand, watch the ocean, I watch it sitting, standing, walking, I walk along its edge with concentration like not stepping on the cracks in sidewalks, or I just tramp through the silky water as it laps up against the sand. I sit on the empty benches on the boardwalk and I watch the ocean. I go to the edge and touch the vastness, the touch of my fingers is then carried back under the water across the earth, and I am immortal: the ocean will carry that touch with it forever. I breathe to the sound of it enduring. I breathe like it does, my blood takes on its rhythms, my heart listens to the sound of the ocean enduring and mimics it.

After five days, my lost boy comes to visit. We swim. In the shower we make love. We sleep on the beach, in the fog, in the mist. Inside the huge slick bugs line the tops of the windows, poised there to drop off or fly, but never moving, primal, they could be gargoyles, guardians in stone but as old as the sea. I watch them. I stare. I am terrified by them but too tired to scream or run or move: I am restless: they sit: I am afraid: they sit: they are long, slick brown things, repulsive, slow: I must be here, near the ocean, or perhaps I will die: maybe they wait for that: grotesque guardians of my lonely, tired death. I am restless. I go inside, I go outside. I listen to music: Bach, Chopin, Mahler, Mozart. They and the ocean are renewal, the will to live. So is the boy, my love, sleeping on the beach. I have left him, fragile, exposed, as I always do, to sleep alone.

He sleeps, I am restless, I go in and out. He leaves the next day. I have two more days here. The ocean has turned me nearly human: closer to life than death. Someday I want the ocean forever, a whole life, day in and day out, a proper marriage: I want to be its human witness: near its magnificence, near the beat of its splendid, terrifying heart. Oh, yes, I am tired: but I have seen the ocean come from the end of the world to touch the sand at my feet.

*

He calls me, the publisher with the dripping upper lip, the hair on it encrusted slightly yellow, slightly green. His voice is melodious, undulating like the ocean, a soft washing up of words on this desolate human shore: a whisper, a wind rushing through the trees bringing a sharp, wet chill. He wants me, wants my book: he is soft, melodious, undulating, tones like music washing up in waves on the shore.

He calls, whispering. You are so wonderful to want me, I say.

*

He calls, whispering, a musical voice, soft, soft, like the ocean undulating or the wind rushing through the trees at dusk, the chill of night in the wind.

I am a writer, I have an agent, she stands between me and every disaster, one human heart with knowledge and skill, some common sense, and I say to her, I cannot stand to talk to him. I don't know what to say to him, I don't know how to say anything to him because anything I say has to mean: take me: have me: I love you: I want you, wonderful you. I knew how, certainly, once. He must be loved, admired, adored, to publish me, whom he now adores. She tells me what to say. I write it down, word for word, on a four-by-six plain index card. I cross out the adjectives. I say what she tells me. I read it, pausing where I have crossed words out. I sound breathy and unsure. ~~Brilliant, brave, heroic~~, you are so wonderful to want me, I say.

*

So wonderful, so wise, so brave, so pure, so true, so smart, so brilliant, so intelligent, so discerning, so unique, so heroic, so honest, so sensitive, so good, so so you are you are.

So kind, so gentle, so tender, so intuitive, so sweet, so fine, so vulnerable, so so you are you are.

The adjectives are all implicit, crossed out on the index cards but whispered under the silence of the dead pauses, massing in clusters under the throat.

*

Tell him, she says, my guardian, my friend, standing between me and disaster, tell him that he alone of all the men in the world has the brilliant and incredibly courageous capacity and talent to . . .

I say that he alone—pause—breathe—breathe—is well I don't say this easily—breathe—breathe—he alone— breathe—pause—breathe—has the—breathy—breathy— talent—pause—

I know, he says, voice undulating.

Oh, I say, breathy, breathy, talent, pause, breathy, breathy, courage, it's so hard for me to, pause, pause, say this, breathe, breathe, but he alone.

I know, he whispers, voice undulating, rushing through the trees, wind at dusk, carrying chill. I know. I will take care of you now, he says, and hangs up.

*

Tell him, she says, this woman who stands between the abyss and me, who believes in me, who year after year stands with me so that I will write, tell him that you trust his judgment implicitly because he is so special and that his incredible mind and phenomenal intellect and brilliant ability to . . .

I say that I trust, I breathe hard, I trust, I pause, I trust him, breathy breathy pause, and his mind is—breathe—breathe— well it's not often that I can honestly say—I breathe—pause, pause—breathy, breathy—his intellect and ability—

I know, he says, breathy, undulating wind rushing.

*

He has to believe that every idea of mine is his. This is the art of being female, but I have lost it. She tells me what to say, I write it down, I cross out the adjectives, I say it, I read it, breathy, full of raw nerves: but in his world the breathy pauses mean fuck me, the misery in my voice means fuck me, the desperate self-effacement means fuck me.

He whispers, undulating: comforts me: he will take care of me now.

*

130

The contracts are signed. I have been breath-fucked, undulated, through several intimate talks on the phone. The phone is slobbered over, whispered over, bits of spit are the silent dissent. In my throat there is a lump the size of a man's fist.

*

My throat has a rock in it, busting the seams of my neck: each breathe-pause-breathe is a word lying down there to die, to decompose, to be a pile of dead bone fragmented in the throat. Each breathy hello, each breathy sentence about he is a hero, he is a rescuer, he is a genius, he is a savior, pulls its way past the rock, bone, graveyard of words not said, remarks not made, a woman's slow death, the familiar silence, the choking, the breathy death. Oh, so quiet, so timid, so wordless, so deferential. It is the only way to absorb, to honor, to recognize, to survive, his ~~immeasurable~~ greatness, his ~~sublime~~ intelligence, his ~~magnificent~~ sensibility, his ~~superbly intuitive~~ understanding. Breathtaking qualities: breathtaking love: of an editor for a writer: of a man for a woman: you are so wonderful, I say. Undulating, he knows.

*

In my throat there is a lump the size of a man's fist. In my throat there is a rock the size of my tears. In my throat unsaid words lie down to die: they are buried there: the writer is dying: the woman is being reborn. Oh, says the breathy little thing, you are so wonderful.

*

The air tries to push past the fist of tears. It comes out in a rush, having had to push through. Oh, says the air having rushed past the swollen lump in the throat, oh—breathe—breathe—pause—a tear silently dies, a word dies—oh, you are so wonderful.

*

His voice undulates, confident, melodious, whispery, I try not to have to talk to him, the phone rings: I have begun already to be afraid: he never says who he is: the undulating voice says *hi*, deep, whispery, melodious, *hi*, *hi*, it sort of slithers out long and slow like a four-syllable word, the inflection going up and down singsong: and he begins talking: it is invariably chivalrous—I thought you would like, I thought you would like to know, I remembered that you like, I protected you from, I saved you from, I remembered that you wanted, I was thinking about you and wanted to know if you wanted—but the voice undulates: like there is some secret: the voice of someone whispering a secret: each time I think it is an obscene phone call but something warns me and I don't hang up, I am courteous and quiet, I listen, and it goes on and on, this undulating voice, and then he says something recognizable, businesslike, but in a deep whisper, and I know it is him, my savior, the one I have to undulate with or die. The phone rings: I have come to dread it: he never says who he is: the voice is melodious, undulating or the wind rushing through the trees at dusk carrying the edge of night, chill, fear. I am breathy, uncertain, timid, tenuous: in his world it means fuck me.

*

Have you ever seen a snake on parched ground, undulating? His voice was like a snake. I am the parched ground.

*

"I can't," I say.

"What will you do then? Where are you going to go?" asks my agent, smart, humane, serious, a serious woman with a serious question. There is nothing to do, nowhere to go.

"I don't know what to say," I say.

"Just say . . ."

I write it down. I cross out the adjectives. I pause. I am breathy. I can barely choke it out. It sounds desperate and sexy. I never have to finish a sentence. "I know," he says, melodious, undulating.

*

The lump in my throat is tears, a fist. It is repulsion, coiled up, ready to spring. Then the wild wires will cut through the silky skin lining the throat and blood will flood the lungs and spill out over the shoulders, and the child will be like a stone statue, ancient marble, desecrated with red paint: head and shoulders cold and polished, throat torn open: Brian DePalma and werewolves: the stone statue on a stand, shoulders and head, eyes empty, no pupils, stone hair matted down in cold ivory: blood tearing out of the torn throat: called *Loved*. I am the child, silent now: a girl sleeping on a bed, it is dark, she is wearing a turquoise dress with old-fashioned buttons all up the front from below the waist to the high neck, and her daddy

comes in to say goodnight, and slowly, slowly, he undoes each
button—she has not been able to sleep, he says go to your room
and just lie down and rest and I will come in, no don't worry
about changing your clothes, so she lies down just as she is, in
her old-fashioned dress with all the buttons—and slowly,
slowly, he undoes each button: it is a dream but she is awake,
a fog, in the dark, she waits, he undoes each button, he is
nervous, throaty, he rubs her, he is throaty, he runs out: the
lump in my throat is tears. I am the child, silent now. It takes
me back that far: that close to annihilation.

*

The phone rings late Friday evening. The whisper goes on and
on. He wants me to come to dinner at his apartment the next
night. I say, well no, I don't think, maybe sometime next week
we could meet, in a restaurant because I know how busy he is.
The whisper deepens, chills. No that really wouldn't be good
because he really wants me to meet this friend of his, a woman
whom he knows I would like very very much and whom I just
absolutely must meet and the problem is that she has been in
Nicaragua with the Sandinistas for the last three months and
she is just back in New York now for a few days and she is
leaving early Monday morning and she and I have so much in
common and the women's struggle in Nicaragua is really so interesting and so essential: he just can't stand to think of her and
me not meeting and he is really just going to be there to cook
dinner: do I like steak? and this is the only chance there is for
me to meet her and find out from someone firsthand, a woman,
you know, more about the situation of women down there. Oh,
yes, well, certainly, I say. I chastise myself for attributing seduction to him. Paranoid, paranoid, I accuse myself. I am nervous and
unhappy: does he or doesn't he: will he or won't he: it doesn't
matter, another woman will be there. Tonight I am safe.

*

Late fall, November already, is blustery, cold. I walk there, to
his apartment, a long walk, an hour, over urban cement,
against a strong wind. Some of the streets are entirely desolate,
deserted. A man offers me $50. I walk fast, against the wind. I
smoke cigarettes one after another. I am on edge, nervous. I
hope to tire myself out, walking miles against the cold wind.

*

The street is dark, deserted. The man lunges out at me and offers me $50. Oh, shit, mister, you have $50 for me. I am put in my place by this stranger, lunging out, I am nervous, on edge: the wind almost knocks me down. The streets are wide. There is no traffic. The streets are dark, deserted. The wind is fierce. I am cold. I am sweating.

*

I find the building where the editor lives. It is on a wide, dark, deserted street, dangerous, deserted. I knock and knock on the heavy wooden door to the lobby. The doorman is elsewhere and there is no other way to get in. I knock and knock, the street is deserted except for the wind, the cold, I almost leave. The doorman opens the door. I go up in the elevator. I am cold. His windows will be closed, his apartment will be warm: it is another world.

*

He is barefoot. The living room is warm. The living room is filled from corner to corner with furniture, three sofas, the three sides of a square, a huge wood table filling the square. The bedroom is just a double bed, the rest of the room empty. There is a tiny dining room with a big round table, set for two. The kitchen is a cubicle, dingy, things hanging everywhere. It is all carpeted. The living room is claustrophobic, there is barely any room for moving, walking, pacing, the three sofas and the wooden table that fills in the space of the square are like one thing, one huge, heavy thing, bedlike. You can get laid anywhere in this room but on the floor. There is a sound system of incredible sophistication: four speakers, two on the floor, two hanging from the ceiling, he can virtually mix his own records by adjusting dials. He has an extra pack of cigarettes there for me, my brand not his. There is a bowl of grass. We sit. He gets me a drink, vodka with ice. He has my brand. He drinks Scotch. I am very nervous. I don't take off my coat. I sit and drink. The whisper of the telephone will not do here. He has to speak up. I am sitting on the far edge of a sofa, as far away as I can get. He is squarely in the middle of the middle sofa. He has his bare feet up on the large square low table that the sofas surround. The sofas and table are inexplicable. I have my coat on. I smoke feverishly. Little philosophers of repression: it is not desire. I am wearing my heaviest motorcycle

134

boots, my plainest black T-shirt, my basic denim, hanging, ragged. He wears denim, a leather belt, a white undershirt. His eyes sort of stare in at his moustache. We smoke. We drink. I am waiting for the woman from Nicaragua. I am hot. I take off my coat. I put it beside me, between him and me, a pile, an obstacle, not subtle. I drink. We chitchat. There is sofa everywhere. One cannot stand or walk around. It is for lying down on. I ask when the woman is coming. Oh, he says, not missing a beat, she just called a while back, I tried to get you but you had left already, she couldn't make it tonight but the next time she is back in the country we will get together, I want you to meet my sister too. A grown-up woman cannot pretend to be a virgin.

*

He knows what I love and what I need and what I do not have. He knows I love music. He knows I live in the cold, in the wind. He knows I haven't been able to buy steak. He puts on music. His record collection is sublime: it is an ecstasy for me: the sound embraces and pierces: his taste is exquisite: he makes me a concert: we don't have to talk: I am happy in the music: he leaves me alone and makes dinner, runs out now and then to change the music, each piece more beautiful, more haunting, more brilliant than the one before it: he knows music: he educates me tastefully and then leaves me to listen. He interrupts to tell me stories about himself, how when he was sick certain pieces of music healed him, the story is long and boring, I listen quietly feigning interest, he will now play those pieces for me: they could make the dead walk: they are the deepest layers of sex, the deepest sensual circles transmuted to formal beauty, ordered, repeated in unspeakably beautiful patterns, sound on sound, sound inside sound, sounds weaved, sounds pulling the body into an involuntary happiness un-related to human time, real life, or narrative detail: sounds deeper than sex: sounds entirely perfect and piercing. He doesn't put on one record and leave it. He changes, weaves, composes, interlaces: just enough, just not quite enough, it leaves you wanting, wanting, needing more.

Dinner is ready, two steaks. We sit next to each other at the big round table. Now he is close enough to whisper. I will tell you, he says, why I am publishing your book, he is whispering, I have to strain closer to hear; I will tell you, he says, whispering, why, the real reason. He is whispering, my ear is almost up against his lips to catch the passing breath, the words just barely discernible on the edge of breathing out. I will tell you, he says, why. Meat juice and fat glisten in his moustache and zing past my ear.

*

He was a schoolboy, probably around fourteen. A teacher and some older boys gang-raped him for hours and cut him up all over with knives.

*

He tells it slowly, detail by detail: the way raped people talk: once one starts the whole story must be told, nothing can be omitted. I see it.

*

I am shaking in pain and rage. I cannot talk. My skin is crawling in terror. I see it.

*

I see it. I see the boy. I see him, the boy, the child. I see him on the table where they did it. I see the torn membranes inside him, the bleeding, the tearing destruction. I see the knife cuts. I feel the pain. I see that he was a child. I see that he was raped. I don't look at the adult male beside me. I shake in pain and rage. I am numb with anger: for him, for us: the raped.

*

He says he sees the man sometimes, the teacher. He says he did the one thing the man would find unbearable: talked to him. He says to me: that's something you will never understand. I say: never. I swear: never. I take an oath: never.

*

I am publishing your book because I know it's true.

*

I am numb. I want to cry but I do not cry. I don't cry over rape any more. I burn but I don't cry. I shake but I don't cry. I get sick to my stomach but I don't cry. I scream inside so that my silent shrieking drowns the awful pounding of my heart but I don't cry. I am too weak to move but I don't cry. I haven't a tear for him. I sit there, immobile, watching the boy on the table. I see him.

*

He clears the table. We go back to the sofas. I sit far away from him. I am quiet: stunned, like from a blow to the head. I sit and stare. That is why, he says. It is more than a pledge: it is a blood oath: he has run our blood together. He has gotten my loyalty: a loyalty above personality, liking, not liking, wanting, not wanting, outside time and daily desires. He puts on Madame Butterfly before she commits suicide. My pain is insane. I do not notice his horrible and cynical wit.

*

I am of course now very gentle with him: in the past I have been harsh but now I know this, I have seen this, the boy, raped, I know why he cares about my writing, it is a secret reason, deep, terrifying: I must treat him with sincerity, respect, like one of us: the raped. I must not hate him for wanting to be close to me anymore. I must not hate him.

*

By now it is 11 pm. I try to go. He keeps me there. There is another story to tell about his parents or his sister. He shows me his bedroom: one night he picked up a baseball team and brought them all back here and got fucked by all of them. I go out of the bedroom to leave. There is another book to discuss. There is another record to hear. He tells me lots of stories about sex, lovers, adventures. I am clear, precise. I am ready to go. There is something he must show me. There is something he must tell me. There is something I must see. There is someone I must meet. I am ready to go. He plays a record by Nichols and May, a couple in bed having just fucked discussing "relating" through prisms of intellectual pretension. It is right on the mark, but we are precoital. I have to go. There is a book he must give me. There is a book he must find. There is a drawing I must see. It is in his bedroom. We stand there together, looking. I have my jacket on. I am like a runner, ready to sprint. There is something he must show me. There is something he must get me. He finds me a long-out-of-print early book by Thomas Mann and a dozen other books, too much for me to carry. I want the books, very much. He finds me a shopping bag. I think about the empty streets. I need my hands free, I don't know if I can find a cab, I leave the books there, I ask him to bring them to his office where I will pick them up. It is 4 am. I run out. I am exhausted and confused. I don't know what he wants. I know what I want: a publisher, not a lover; a publisher, not a barter. I think he wants me but I

137

insist to myself I am me, not a woman, the signs are no longer in my symbology, I do not speak that language, I do not practice that religion: I have seen him, a child, gang-raped, cut with knives, it is why he wants to be near me, I am required by my own dumb heart to love him, he is one of us, the raped, I do not have to sleep with him, surely that is not what he meant.

*

I know what he wanted, he wanted me to ask to see the scars, to run my fingers over them, to love him because of them, to stay there, touching the scars, while he bit and clawed and screwed. I have seen such scars. Of course, I knew what he wanted: old habits: familiarity, the smell, the language of the body: you run your hands over scars like that and you stay the night.

*

I get home. The windows are open. The wind blows through. I am so cold.

*

I don't want him. I need him, oh desperately, but I don't want him. I have his secret, sorrow added to sorrow, pain added to pain, rape added to rape. I am faithful to the raped, it is my only fidelity. I have his secret. It was a blood oath but not on my blood, my real blood, so it is not enough, I know that, he is a man, he needs my real blood, my blood is the blood beyond symbol, uterine blood, vaginal blood, seasonal blood, stench blood, strong blood; it is not over because it has not been my blood, him cutting, me bleeding, the way a man and woman do it. Others say: oh, he is gay, don't worry, he doesn't want *that*. Others say: oh, don't be silly, he can't want *that*. Oh, he can't want *that*. I want to buy it. He can't want *that*. The raped don't do that to the raped, I want to believe.

*

Others say: oh, don't be silly, he can't want *that*. I am dense, troubled but dense. Before I knew what he wanted and how he wanted it, but now I am blinded, because the raped don't do that to the raped. I decide: he can't want *that*. I don't believe it really, but others say he can't want *that*, so I don't really know what he wants, not *that*, I say. I pick a posture: he has told me a secret: we are colleagues with a special understanding: his secret: I will be patient and loyal because of his secret: because I hurt in his behalf. I am always astonished by the cruelty of

138

rape. I am awed by the enduring of it. I am awed by those who carry the secret: those bodies carrying it, burned in; those minds collapsing under the weight of vivid recollection that doesn't pale with time. I am awed by the intensity of the never-assuaged anguish. I am confused. I don't know what he wants from me. He can't want *that*. In private, I am troubled. In public I am dense; we are colleagues with a special understanding.

*

I feel dread, confusion, panic: he can't want *that*. *That* is so simple and this whole routine is so complex. I need him but I don't want him. I am cold, the wind blows through the apartment, I am destitute and I have nowhere left to go: I don't know what to do except to walk away: and I can't do that because I am too desperate and he is one of the raped.

*

I have nowhere else to go. I have no money, no hope of being published elsewhere, by anyone else, my work offends everyone else. Life is dead ends, ghostly alleys. I need him. I am so confused, so cold, unhappy. I don't know what he wants. Others say: not *that*. I think: well, it can't be *that*.

*

Underneath, inchoate—it is *that*. I want him to stay away. I know he is coming closer.

*

I even say to myself: just do it. Just do it. But I don't want to. I say to myself: just do it, in the long run it will be so much simpler, get it over with, just do it, he will get tired of you soon, what difference can it make to you, one more or less— but it makes a difference, I don't know why, I don't even want it to: it just does. I am cold and I am tired and I don't want to.

*

I am confused, but he is not. It boils over: he loves me. I am scorched by it everywhere I turn, in private, in public, in the little world of business where I go to meet with him, the little world of huge skyscrapers and sterile offices. Like sunlight, it blazes. I don't know what it is or why or what it consists of—but there is no missing it—I am his special someone or something: he emanates it: it is no secret: every secretary and office boy treats me like his bride. I like being loved. He is no fool. I like being loved: so much so that I want

139

to be loved more: and more: and more. I like it when men love me. I especially like it when it starts to make them hurt. I like it when they hurt. I am hooked enough. I am a player in the game.

*

Nevertheless I do not want it. I am proper, distant. I am formal. I am soft-spoken: in his world it means fuck me.

*

The phone rings. His voice slithers. There is some detail of production. I am called into his office. I am treated like the Queen of Sheba. Everyone is both warm and deferential, respectful, amused by my jokes, I am never left waiting, I am escorted, welcomed, not just by secretaries and office boys. The president of the company introduces himself to me, shakes my hand, welcomes me: more than once. I am singled out: the beloved.

I go in prepared not to take up time. I am there four hours later, six hours later. Everyone has gone home. We sit alone high up in the sky surrounded by dusk. It gets dark. We walk out. We walk along the sidewalks. We come to where he turns to go to his apartment. I hold out my hand for a formal handshake. He draws me close and kisses me. I walk on, alone.

*

If I have to call him, I try to leave a message, take care of it indirectly: I talk to my agent and ask her to call him. He always has me come in. I go in with a list: the things that must be taken care of. I pull out the list and say: this is a list. I cross things off the list as we discuss them. It is never less than four hours, six hours. I try to get it done. He must tell me this and that. He loads me down with gifts: books. They are cheap gifts from a publisher, but nevertheless: they are special, precious, what I love, not thrown at me but given carefully, in abundance, he introduces me to new writers, he gives me beautiful books, he thinks about what I like and what I don't like. He keeps me there. My list sits. We walk out together. We get to the corner. I go to shake his hand. He kisses me fervently. I walk on, alone.

*

He takes me to dinner, it is the same. Romantic. He talks. I try to end it. He talks on and on. I shake his hand. He kisses me. I walk on, alone.

*

The meetings go on for months. I go to his office. He keeps me there. Everyone leaves. He tells me sexy stories, his lovers, his adventures. I have my list out. He talks about writers. He gives me books. He talks about himself, endless. It is dusk. It is dark. There is a sofa in his office. He brings me over there. I don't sit down. I keep standing. I am formal. We walk out together. We walk several blocks together. He does not acknowledge any of my moves to go. Finally, I go to shake his hand. He pulls me. He kisses me. I walk on, alone.

*

It is dark. It is night. We walk several blocks together. It is time for him to turn off to his apartment. I don't shake his hand. I start to move away fast, almost running, and say good-bye once I am moving away. He grabs me and pulls me and kisses me. I walk on, alone.

*

I dread the meetings, always four hours, six hours. Every smile is a lie. He publishes my book with some money behind it, a token of his esteem like a fine piece of jewelry would be. The book is savaged. I am humiliated, ashamed. It keeps him away. It is the one good thing. He could probably have me now. I am too ashamed to pull away. He could wipe his dick on me now. Why not?

*

He bought the next book before this savaged one was published. It was a token of his esteem, like a fine piece of jewelry would be.

I work feverishly to meet my deadline. I have one year. He leaves me alone. I am desperate for money. The landlord sets up a new exhaust system for the restaurant downstairs. The windows are closed. I am still cold all the time but the windows are closed. I am afraid I will suffocate, that the air is still poison, but I am too cold to open the windows. Sometimes the new exhaust system doesn't work and I get sick so I am nervous and afraid each day but the windows are closed. Sometimes they are opened for a week at a time because the new exhaust system doesn't work but most of the time the windows are closed. Each day I beat down the humiliation of the last book to work on this new one: it is like keeping vomit from coming up. I work hard. A year passes. I finish it. He has called to assure me of his love but he leaves me alone.

*

Then the rats come. Just as I am finishing, the rats come. There are huge thuds in the walls, heavy things dropping in the walls, great chases in the ceiling, they are right behind the plaster, chasing, running, scrapping. The walls get closer and closer, Edgar Poe knew a thing or two, the room gets smaller and smaller. I am up each night and they are running, falling, dropping, chasing, heavy, loud, scampering, fast. They are found dead in the halls. The landlord says they are squirrels.

*

Night after night: they drop like dead weight in the walls, they run in the ceiling, the walls close in, the ceiling drops down, plaster falls, they are running above the bed, they are running above the bath, they are running above the sink, the toilet, the sofa, the desk, they are in the walls, falling like dead weight, we put huge caches of poison in great holes we make in the walls, we plaster the holes, sometimes one dies and the stink of the rotting carcass is inescapable, vomitous, and still they run and chase and fall and pounce: they are overhead and on every side. I am scared to death and ready to go mad, if only God would be good to me.

*

I live like this for months. The publisher has promised to publish a secret piece of fiction only he has read. He read it months before, in the privacy of his love for me. Now I have submitted it officially. He has promised me, money, everything. I am entirely desperate for money. I am so afraid. He knows about the rats. He knows how poor I am. He knows I am ready to leave the sleeping boy, who sleeps through the jumping and chasing and great dull thuds. I am, frankly, too desperate and too tired to love. I am too afraid. The boy sleeps. I do not. This constitutes—finally—an irreconcilable difference.

The editor tells my agent he must talk to me about structure: ideas he has for the piece of fiction: this means he will publish it, but he has these ideas I must listen to.

I call to make an appointment at his office.

He insists on dinner.

There is dinner, coffee afterward: a restaurant, a coffeehouse. He talks and talks and talks. I drink and drink and drink. I am waiting for the ideas about structure. He orders for me. He smothers me with talk. I drink more. I ask in the restaurant about his ideas about structure. He ignores me and keeps talking. I drink. He talks about sex. He talks about his life. He talks about his lovers. I say: well we must get absolutely sober now so I can hear your ideas about structure. We go to a coffeehouse. He talks. He talks about how he has to love an author. He talks about the authors he has loved. He talks about someone he is involved with who is writing a novel: he talks about visiting this author and that author and what they drink and how they love him and how they want him. I say I want to hear his ideas about structure. He tells me he is going to buy a beach house, a house by the ocean, where I can come to live and write. He says he has found it. He says it is right on the ocean. He says he can picture me there, working, undistracted, not having to worry about fumes and rats and poverty. He tells me that as long as he has a home I have a home and that this home, on the ocean, is very special and for me. He knows it is what I have always wanted, more than anything: it is my idea of peace and solace. I say thank you but I had a rather strange childhood always being moved from home to home because my mother was sick sort of like an orphan and I am not too good about staying in other people's houses. I ask him about his ideas about the structure of the novel. He says that his involvement with the work of an author and his involvement with the author are indistinguishable, he has to love them as one. He tells me about the house he is buying right on the ocean where I will go and work and finish the novel. He tells me he sees me in it working. I ask him about his ideas about structure. He tells me that he wants me to understand that now I have a home, with him, by the ocean, he has bought a home there where I will live and write, his home and my home. We leave the coffeehouse. We get to the corner where we go in different directions. I ask him if he wants to tell me about his ideas about structure so I can think about them. He tells me that the publishing company is my home too, as long as he is there, and he wants me to see the house on the ocean which is my home: and the publishing house is my home, because wherever he is is my home. He tells me to call him, day or night. He tells me to call him at home. I look blank, because I am blank; I am blank. He kisses me. I walk away, alone. He calls after me: remember you have a home now. I met him at six for dinner, it is now three in the morning, I don't know his ideas on structure. I walk home, alone. The rats are in the walls. The walls are closing in. Someone, a stranger, blond, six feet, muscled, curled in fetal position, is sleeping. I do not call the publisher, no, I don't, I wait for his offer of money on my novel. Months go by. I don't call him, my agent keeps calling him, he says he is working on it, trust him, six or seven months go by, the stranger in the next room and I barely speak to each other, the rats are monstrous, I am hungry. I say to my agent: you must find out, I must have money. She calls. He says he doesn't do fiction. He doesn't do fiction. My book that I finished when the rats came is published a few months later. He lets it die, no gift like jewelry for me anymore. He preordains its death and it dies. I see my house, the ocean so near it. I see the beach, smooth wet sand, and the curve of the waves on the earth, the edge of the ocean, so delicate, so beautifully fine, lapping up on the beach like slivers of liquid silver. I see the sun, silver light on the winter water, and I see dusk coming. I am alone there, in winter, ice on the sand, silver waves outside the window. I see a small, simple house, white and square against the vast shore. I see the simple beauty of the house absorbing the dusk, each simple room turning somber, and then the dusk reaching past the house onto the wet beach and finally spreading out over the ocean. I see the moon over the ocean. I see the night on the water. I see myself in the simple house, at a window, looking out, just feeling the first chill of night. I sit in the apartment, rats are running in the walls, the walls are closing in, writing my poor little heart out: in a terrible hurry to tell what is in my heart. You have to be in a terrible hurry or the heart gets eaten up. There is a carcass, sans heart, writing its little heart out so to speak: in a terrible hurry: and somewhere an ocean near a house, waiting. He can't want *that*, they said, oh no, not *that*. I am a writer, not a woman, I thought somewhere down deep, he can't want that. Now I am in a terrible hurry to tell what is in my heart. Who could hurry fast enough? *Brava!* whoever managed it!

Did I remember to say that I always wanted to be a writer, since I was a little girl?